LOCKE OUT

The Collected Writings of

Richard Locke

Illustrations by Robert W. Richards

FIRSTHAND BOOKS

LOCKE OUT: THE COLLECTIVE WRITINGS OF RICHARD LOCKE is an original publication of FirstHand Books. This work has never before appeared in book form, although some of the stories and essays appeared originally in *Stallion, Advocate Men, Drummer, Friction, FirstHand, Manscape,* and *Guys* magazines. Any similarity to actual persons or events is purely coincidental.

Published by:

> FirstHand Books
> 310 Cedar Lane
> Teaneck, NJ 07666

Cover photo by Rink Foto.
Illustrations by Robert W. Richards
Design and typography by Laura Allen

ISBN: 0-943383-06-4

PRINTED IN CANADA

Many of the activities described in *Locke Out* have long been considered dangerous, and in light of the current AIDS crisis they could prove lethal today. The author and the publishers do not recommend that the reader attempt to duplicate them.

CONTENTS

❖ THE STORIES ❖

❖ THE ESSAYS ❖

THE
STORIES

❖ ❖ ❖ ❖ ❖ ❖

THE
CORNFIELD

❖ ❖ ❖ ❖ ❖ ❖

The
Cornfield

❖ ❖ ❖ ❖ ❖

Dave Sullivan set his hoe down. It was the unusually heavy, vernal heat that made the sweat pour off his back and chest and drip down into his pants. He walked over to the shade tree, picked up the jug of water, and took a swallow. He looked over into the cornfield for Jack O'Hara before he sat down. As he sat there, he knew he was going to have to find Jack. It was quiet there under the tree. Only the sounds of the birds and insects could be heard. It was nice for Dave to sit awhile.

Jack's father was a hard taskmaster. And with the sudden quiet of not hearing their hoes in the weeds, Mr. O'Hara would be looking for both of them. Jack had been slow in his work and chores lately, and Dave had covered for him. Dave knew it was the spring heat; he felt it himself, but he couldn't shield Jack's spring fever anymore. Mr. O'Hara had made that clear to Dave last night. Now Dave was feeling sorry for the tongue-lashing he had given Jack this morning.

"For all the good it did—the little fucker's gone again," Dave said out loud as he stood up, walked around the far edge of the cornfield, and took the path to the river. "That little fucker is big enough to give me quite a fight. He's as tall as me, but a bit lean."

Along the river bank, he could smell the willows. Mr. O'Hara was too strict with the kid. The bitterness of the old man had instilled him with the forgetfulness of spring fever.

"God knows what makes him so bitter. Well, that's no worry of mine," Dave said to himself.

As he turned a curve in the path, he found Jack lying on the sandy riverbank. Jack had just gone for a swim and was lying nude on the shore. His reddish-blond hair still dripped river water. His chest rose and fell, revealing the good musculature of a very young man/boy, rippling from the work of years raised on the farm and exertion of hoeing the fields. This morning as Dave looked upon the young man, Dave's cock began to get hard. He had thought he would eventually get over the effect the boy had on him. He had never even thought of it until these last few months, when the spring had revealed the boy's growth into manhood. They both went to the river for a swim every day before supper. Over and over again, he noticed that boy's cock and cockhead had reached the length of full manhood.

Standing there, looking down on the young man, Dave's thoughts wandered a bit. Dave was feeling good about things. He had finally worked off his indenture last fall. He was a free man working his way West. Mr. O'Hara had hired Dave last winter before the spring thaw. His indenture had been five long years. The passage from Ireland had cost him dearly. This was the Spring of 1836 and his first year of freedom. Dave could have the money saved by fall for the passage to St. Louis or maybe even Texas. Out in the wilds, a man could be free. He wouldn't be anybody's hired hand or have to step aside for any man.

The hard cock in his pants brought Dave back to the river and Jack lying there in front of him. Dave's cock felt the rising heat of spring and had been increasingly insistent lately. He was jacking off more and more to release the tensions built up during the warm spring days. It had been a long time since he had fucked anything. That whore in Buffalo had been the last, and that was last autumn.

Now, the lust of spring gripped him. Now, he was angry with the kid for slowing down the workday. Now, he could get fired because of this kid.

"Come on, Jack!" Dave yelled to the kid. "It's time to get back to the field before your father misses us. Come on, get your ass up the trail!"

Dave's yell startled Jack from his reverie. He was enjoying the warm sun on his river-cooled body. The water had cooled his body but not his cock. At first, the river had shrunk his cock and balls into his body, but now his cock was half-hard from the warmth of the sun and the warmth of his thoughts about the man yelling at him. He had been thinking of Dave. Reluctantly, he got up.

"Okay, I'm coming. Let me get my pants on." Jack stood up and bent over to pick up his pants. "You gonna take a swim?"

"Yes, I'll be right there. Now you get your ass up to the cornfield."

After Jack left, Dave took off his pants and dived into the water. The icy river cooled off his cock and Dave lost his hard-on.

After his swim, Dave thought the hard-on that had been with him all morning would go away. He had recently begun fantasizing about fucking with this young man. He had always held back from the kid, not because of any moral qualms, but because Jack had never let him know that he was open for that kind of friendship. Dave wasn't sure how open he was himself. He had never—except for that one time when he was a kid—been with another male. But Jack haunted him.

They worked side by side. Sometimes Mr. O'Hara would

be there, too, and for the most part they all got on well. Mr. O'Hara, though, was beginning to get to Dave. His harsh treatment of the young man was for the most part uncalled for.

"That fucker!" Dave said out loud as he grabbed his hoe from under the tree where he had left it. He could barely see Jack at the other end of the field, although the kid's head would occasionally pop up over the top of the tall corn. Dave started work where he had left off.

The sweat began to ooze from his pores. Again, it was soaking his waistband, dripping onto his boots. His cock was beginning to harden again as the monotony of the hoeing turned his thoughts to the young man.

"God, he was so beautiful lying there on the sand," he muttered to himself.

The lean body, tanned by the sun, radiantly reflected his youth. The hair around his cock and balls was fuzzy and only slightly darker than the sun-streaked hair on his head. Dave's hard cock was again insistent. He put his hoe down and un-buttoned his pants, pulling out his cock. He grabbed it with both hands and squeezed. His cock was now rockhard, and the intense pressure of his hands did no good. It hurt and felt good at the same time. He took it out and began to stroke it, slowly at first, then faster. He spit onto his right hand and began to pull the skin fast and hard over the swollen head. It swelled even more. It felt so good. . .it felt so good. Dave reached into his mind and pulled back the image of Jack's cock lying on his thigh, half-hard and bobbing in the sunlight. Dave's cock had throbbed when Jack had bent over to pick up his pants back at the river, with that young asshole peering at him from across the sand. Dave's cock throbbed even more in thinking back at that sight. He began to pull on his cock, jerking harder and harder.

The more he pulled and jacked, the more hard and swollen his cock became. Within moments, his cum shot out and over the upturned hoe. Dave let go his pent-up breath and released a large volume of air from his lungs, as he suppressed a cry in his throat.

"God, this kid is gonna bust my gut," Dave thought. He breathed in deeply and sighed.

Early the next day, Dave was throwing hay down to the cows when Jack came into the barn and yelled up to him. Dave climbed down the ladder.

"Hi, Jack—how's your mornin'?"

Jack didn't look good. He was upset, angry.

"What's the matter? Your father gettin' to ya again?"

The kid shook his head. "I can't handle this anymore. I don't know what to do."

Dave looked across to Jack, right into his eyes. "Well, kid, I'm sorry, but I can't help you. He's your father. It's your problem."

Jack had held all this back for years, for he had never had anybody to talk with. As he had come to know Dave, though, he had begun to hope that maybe Dave could help him out of this. Lately, he had even hoped that Dave would take him away from the hell of this farm and his angry father.

"Dave, can I go with you this fall?" he asked.

Dave sighed and said, "I told you—you're gonna have to handle it yourself. You're gonna have to learn to be your own man. Better now than later."

Disappointed, Jack nodded sadly. "I suppose you're right. I just don't know what I'm gonna do." Jack took a deep breath and turned toward the door. He stopped for a second, turned, and walked up to his friend. "Dave, I saw you in the cornfield jerking off yesterday. I've seen you doin' things all this spring down at the river. I've worked by your side every day—and, well, I want more." Jack reached across and kissed Dave. "I love you and I can't handle that, either."

Dave wasn't startled enough to back off from the kid, but it did take him a moment to return the affection. Jack was about to pull back from Dave and start to apologize, but Dave stopped him with a kiss of his own. Jack threw himself into the man and opened his mouth for Dave's tongue. Not holding back a thing, Dave pulled the young man into him. He didn't have time to reflect on the suddenness of what was happening. He moved his arms down Jack's back and onto the firm young buttocks of the boy and pulled the bulging crotch into his. Their hard cocks pressed into each other. Dave opened the kid's shirt, grabbed his chest, and began to pinch his tits. He opened his mouth and Jack stuck his tongue in. Dave opened Jack's pants while Jack pulled at Dave's belt. Soon, they were standing naked in front of one another. They pushed together, bringing their cocks up to stand opposite one another on their bellies. Dave grabbed Jack's hand and led him to the other end of the barn and into the tack room where Dave made his bunk. They found the hard, single bed, and Dave took hold of the kid's ass. Jack raised his legs and guided Dave's cock to where he knew it was gonna hurt, but he was ready for the hurt.

As Dave's bigness entered him, Jack relaxed into the reverie that had consumed him all this spring. He opened himself to this man, to the hugeness entering him, and gave Dave his ass, his body, and his love. For too many years he had held himself in check. Now he let himself go. He had known only hatred from his father, never any love. Now Dave was inside him. He had Dave; that was all he wanted. Four months ago Dave had come into his life, and in that time Jack had changed. He had never given a thought to the consequences of the feelings he had for Dave. The love had built up over the last few months until he couldn't hold it in. Now, it came pouring out of him. Dave, he knew, was feeling the same. Dave's cock in his ass only accentuated the feelings, the physical sensations. The arms around him encircled his body and his love.

Dave fell into the overwhelming abyss of the young man and plunged his cock deeper into him. The kid's cock was lying across his belly. Dave reached down, spit on his hand, and began to stroke it. Jack felt hard love in his ass, and all up and down his cock, he felt the man's rough hands. He looked at Dave and then to where Dave's loins were driving into him, and then back into Dave's eyes.

"Oh, God, I love him. I love him in me. I love working beside him. I love to look at the big man while he works or while he's lying in the shade of a tree," Jack said to himself while looking into the green eyes of the man who was pushing and pulling inside him.

Jack yelled, he moaned, and he sighed. The big man's cock stroked the inside of his ass and his big hand stroked the outside of his cock. Jack shot straight into the air as he yelled, and again when he moaned, and then again when he sighed. He arched his back, wrapped his legs around Dave, and yelled again. Another load greater than the first shot into Dave's face.

Then, suddenly, another voice echoed through the barn.

"You fucking bugger! You whore fucker! I'm gonna shoot your ass all over the side of the barn!" Mr. O'Hara yelled from the doorway of the tack room, then turned and ran out of the barn toward the house.

Dave had come when Jack shot that last load, and his head was still reeling from it. He shook his head. He was not thinking clearly. Then it came to him what had happened. By now, Mr. O'Hara was no doubt halfway to the house. Both he and Jack had no time to think. He stood up, bent down and kissed Jack, then ran out of the barn and into the corral. He grabbed Mr. O'Hara's horse and jumped on. Jack had followed him and opened the gate. Mr. O'Hara stood on the porch with the shotgun raised to his shoulder. He fired, but was too far from the corral, and the buckshot merely stung the naked men. Mr. O'Hara jumped off the porch and began running toward them. Dave looked down at Jack from the horse and reached out toward the boy. Jack looked up to him and without a second thought or a glance at his father, reached up and jumped on behind his man. Naked, they gallopped out of the corral and out onto the post road. They heard one more shot but were now even farther away. Dave turned and kissed Jack, threw his head back, and laughed. Jack joined in his laughter.

At the sight of both of them laughing madly, galloping naked down the road, Mr. O'Hara threw down his gun. ▼

❖ ❖ ❖ ❖ ❖ ❖ ❖

THE
TOMBSTONE

❖ ❖ ❖ ❖ ❖ ❖ ❖

The
Tombstone

❖ ❖ ❖ ❖ ❖

Inside the graveyard at Mission Dolores, the oldest in San Francisco, the city of Saint Francis, stands a tombstone with the following inscription:

SACRED TO THE MEMORY OF THE LATE DECEASED
JAMES SULLIVAN
AGED 45 YEARS
DIED BY THE HANDS OF THE VC
(VIGILANTE COMMITTEE)
MAY 31, 1856
AGE 45 YEARS
ANTHEM
Remember not, O Lord, Our offences, Nor Those Of Our
Parents, Neither take thou vengeance of our sins. Thou
shalt bring Soul Out Of Tribulation And In thy Mercy Thou
Shalt Destroy Mine Enemies
A Native Of Brandon, Ireland
ERECTED BY JAMES MULLOY
JANUARY 26, 1858

The following story has nothing at all to do with the facts concerning the two men mentioned on the tombstone. It is a fantasy created the time I first stood in front of that tombstone. This is not a true story and concerns no one living or dead. It's a bit of drama, a bit of comedy, a bit of pathos. It is heroic at times and dedicated to the spirit which first set stick to tablet, brush to canvas. It is, in short, merely a passing fancy.

It had been a long trail for Jim and Jimmy. They had come a long way since they had set sail from Belfast. Twenty-five years had passed since the armory had blown up in their faces. They had been to New Orleans, they had plied the Mississippi, they had seen the travesty at the Alamo, and had gone deep into the mountains where Jim had become a *shaman* with the Sioux. Now they were drifting into California and the gold country. Jimmy had grown into a middle-aged man who now called himself James. Jim was only a few years older than James, and they both still had their youth and vigor, for the rugged years had taught them both how to survive in a harsh frontier world. In their younger days, they were wanted men. Their days as freedom fighters were long gone, and the bitter memories of the dead and dying had diminished with time.

With regard to a hanging offense, whether it be for buggery or for stealing horses, the rope hangs just as straight for either crime. And so, they had changed their last names and had become fairly solid citizens. But they still dared not go east of the Mississippi. They had robbed too many gamblers, too many bankers.

They had drifted into Texas before the Republicans revolted against Mexico. They had eagerly joined the Republicans, but after a fighting skirmish, they had both deserted Texas and gone into the Rockies. They weren't cowardly—they just couldn't kill men. Over the years they had been together, they had met many men and loved most of them, in and out of the sack.

In the Rockies, the two men had become trappers. For five years, the men had trapped beaver. They had reached the headwaters of the Mississippi and had gone as far as the Columbia River. During these five years, the yearly meetings at the flats were the only signs of civilization they saw. The meetings were raucous—up to three or four thousand men would come together in the spring and trade their pelts for the supplies they needed. The shindig would last all May. The drinking, the dancing, and the spirits of men—friends as well as enemies coming together—could be explosive.

The yellow apron, used to designate the "female" partner for reels and such, was passed from dancer to dancer and was supposed to alleviate most of the tensions. More often, however, the apron could create a few. Jim and James had both worn the apron. Both had been caught in the middle of a few of the fights. Not often, though. They had long ago decided that they would rather be caught between blankets than knives. All the fun wasn't confined to the dancing area.

In loving one another, they had come to love all men, all men who were honest with their dealings as well as their feelings. These trappers had reasons to be in this lawless country where only friends trusted one another.

Jim and James had counted *coup* with their brothers, the Olgala Sioux, against the Blackfoot. They had been very brave. The cowardice they had seemed to show in Texas was not present with the Sioux. They had counted *coup*, come up to enemy warriors, and touched them with their weapons. It wasn't necessary to kill to count *coup*. They had spent many years in the mountains with their friends, the trappers and the Sioux.

The odyssey of the two men over twenty-five years finally brought them to the Gold Coast of California. All the gold fields in Alta, California were staked out. Jim and James searched as far north as Oregon, and then turned south, into Baja country, looking for new strikes. With no luck. That was when they decided to look closer at the gold fields around Sonora.

The trail from Los Angeles had been dusty. They had come up to old King's Highway, the "El Camino Real," and were camping at Land's End, just outside the City of Saint Francis. It was now, in 1855, a bustling American community.

As the sun set, they washed the trail dirt off their bodies with the surf, then set up camp for the night to rest before they started into town the next morning.

Over the years, the excitement of that long ago early morning hiding out in the shepherd's hut in the low mountains outside of Belfast had grown more intense for the two men. Since that moment of discovery, the manhood of James sheathed in his foreskin and the manhood of Jim were irrevocably entwined about each other. For Jim, life without James didn't exist.

Jim walked over to the woodpile he had built, picked up some of the sticks he and James had gathered at dusk, and threw them on the fire. He looked up as James walked into the firelight with a rabbit hanging from his belt.

"Sorry it took so long. The sunset was so beautiful on the cliff, I just had to sit and watch it sink into the ocean."

Jim had grown to know the beauty of the younger man who, after all these years, was still getting lost in his reveries. It was either the beauty of men or the beauty of the country. Hell, for that matter, he loved the beauty of the Universe. The sun, moon, and the stars had been their roof for over twenty-five years. The adventures shared by the two men had made them inseparable, and they could go for days not saying a word.

Jim was quickly brought out of his thoughts as James moved swiftly from the firelight into the night with his gun drawn, motioning for Jim to be silent. Just then, a cry from the *arroyo*, and the whinny of a horse broke the stillness of the early night darkness.

"*Conyo. Ayuda, caballeros, Ayuda.*"

Jim reached down and picked up a firebrand and looked into the *arroyo*. There, at the bottom, was a horse standing riderless. Its rider lay on the ground, holding his bleeding head. Jim scampered down the trail, grabbed the horse, and tethered it to a tree. If the man were hurt badly, the horse would be needed. San Francisco wasn't far, and the man could be taken there for help.

"*¿Habla ingles?*" asked Jim, who knew a bit of Spanish.

In the light of the firebrand, the young Mexican looked small and wiry. He stood up, showing that he had not been hurt that badly.

"Yes, Senor, I speak English," the young Mexican replied. "I saw your campfire and was heading for it when my horse lost his footing and we both came down the side of the *arroyo*. Ahheee, my head hurts."

"Here, let me look at it," offered Jim. The wound was jagged and ran across the hairline above the youth's eye. "You're gonna have quite a nice scar across your forehead, but it looks like there's been no real damage to your head. Come to the fire and my partner will take care of you. He's spent some time with a *shaman of* the Sioux—he knows medicine."

As they came into the firelight, Jim yelled to James.

"It's okay—only a wounded man here. Get out your medicine kit."

As they sat down, Jim picked up more wood, adding it to the fire so that James could see what he was doing. In the firelight, the Mexican was quite handsome. Jim breathed heavily at the sight of him and exchanged a glance with James. They were each impressed by the man. He was a small package with explosives written on it, from the look of him.

James brought the medicine kit from his saddlebag and began to work on the Mexican's head. The man stifled a gasp as James applied a poultice he'd made of herbs mixed with bear grease. He then wrapped the stranger's forehead with a clean cloth torn from an old white shirt.

"Well, that should fix you, *amigo*. This gentleman here is Jim, and I'm James." For a long moment, James peered at the Mexican's face. "That sure is a nasty cut, but I think the poultice will help it. In fact, the way I put the skin back, you might not even be scarred, but if it does, it should lend a lot of character. You're a handsome man, and a scar will only make you that much more attractive."

"*Gracias, amigo*. My name is Alejandro Guerrero. I am embarrassed. The fall, it was a stupid thing, no?"

"I'm glad we were able to help," replied James.

Alejandro looked sheepishly at both of them. "I was on my way to send you *gringos* away from the *ranchero*. The Don no longer allows the *gringos* to pass over his land. You can stay the night if you promise you will leave in the morning. The Don will have to know about you anyway." Suddenly, before he could continue, he winced. "Aiiee, my head is pounding!"

James brought a canteen filled with a potion he had mixed for him. It was a heady drink that would relieve the pain. The *shaman* had given James the recipe for the potion and instructed him in its use. The drink was made of herbs and a red-tinged mushroom that grows in early spring and sometimes in late fall rains.

James smiled. Jim saw James smile. Both knew that the young man's head would stop pounding in a moment, replaced by a pounding asshole and a throbbing cock.

The *shaman* and James had had a good time of it when they'd first made the potion. Jim didn't see James and the *shaman* for almost two weeks. That had been the longest time he had ever spent away from Jim. James had missed being with Jim. Though he was learning, he had reluctantly said good-bye to the *shaman* . Through the years, Jim and James had used the drink many times, and not only for medicinal purposes.

The young man was no longer complaining about his head and seemed almost in a torpor. James knew it would only be a few more moments before the erotic effects would begin.

Jim looked over at James and said, "Well, you've done it again, haven't you? Do we have enough for two more?"

"Comin' right up," James replied.

Jim began to take off his clothes. In the firelight, his body began to reveal itself. The leather shirt came off first, showing the expansive chest of the older man. The hair, black and curly, sprinkled liberally with gray, sprang in tufts around his nipples. The line from the mid-chest spread across and down his belly to the depths below his belt. Jim shucked his Levi's as James brought the canteen.

The young Mexican looked up at Jim in the firelight. The pain in his head was gone. Jim raised the cup to his lips and drank it to the bottom while James followed suit. The young man stood up and came between Jim and James. James stepped away and began to take off his clothes while the young man dropped to his knees and began to suck on Jim's cock.

The mushrooms were already working on Jim and James. Knowing the effects, they both used the drink to increase the excitement they had felt when the firelight had revealed the handsomeness of the young man now sucking on Jim's cock.

Alejandro, not missing a beat, began to pull off his clothes, too. The fire shed its light onto the three men as they splayed themselves on the ground around the fire. James picked up the Mexican's ass as Alejandro sucked on Jim's cock, and stuck his face into the asscheeks and ran his tongue into the asshole of the young man. At the same time, the Mexican impaled his head on Jim's cock and then backed up onto James' tongue.

Jim looked down into James' eyes. His eyes had gone back into his head, and now James was aware only of his tongue and his own cock in his hands. Jim pulled his cock out of Alejandro and went around to the back of James, grabbed the bear grease out of the medicine kit, and rubbed some on his cock and then onto James' asshole.

For Jim, it was always like the first time. It was always new and always good, always the same as that fucking, gut-busting first time. In all the years, and all the men, he had never gotten over how good it is to fuck a man. Jim had never experienced this kind of excitement with women. For over twenty years he had been fucking men.

"And they fucked me good as well," Jim said to himself.

James had always been with him, and while Jim was getting buttfucked, James would fuck his face. James had fucked him that night when they had been so scared, when they had scampered through the streets of Belfast. They had become inseparable after that night. As far as Jim knew, James had never been with any other man, except for those they had later shared in their bunkroll.

Sometimes it was a real fight to get on the bottom. Like that big trapper, Ole. He was so big. His arms were as big as Jim's thighs. It would have been a great fight.

"We fucked that man good," Jim said to himself. "Aw, hell, though, it's good. Cock, balls, ass, tits, mouths, all of it. A man, any man. With James and me, it doesn't matter. We like them all."

By this time, Alejandro was being pumped with James' cock and James in turn was being fucked himself by Jim. Jim's asshole was empty and needed filling. He pulled his cock out of James and went out to the front of Alejandro. Jim raised Alejandro to a standing position and then in the firelight he bent over in front of the man. Alejandro needed no urging. He spit first onto his cock and then onto Jim's ass, and pushed right in. When this fuck had first started, Jim had not paid attention to the little bugger's manhood, but now, as Jim looked back through his legs, he saw the Mexican's cock. It appeared to be over a foot long and was coming right for his ass. In response, Jim threw his body back and plunged his ass onto the shaft of the cock. It entered Jim's asshole and went straight in, to the hilt.

Alejandro was being used by James to fuck his lover; Alejandro was only the medium. Squeezed in the middle like that, he got very excited. His whole being became his cock. Alejandro's ass felt like an extension of Jim's ass; his cock felt like an extension of James' cock. Caught up in the excitement of both men, Alejandro added his own energy to the bucking and fucking. Jim grabbed his own hard cock and began to pound it with his big fist in time to the buggering by Alejandro and James. Jim came, and the thunder that filled his body spurted into the fire. It was the Mexican coming into his ass that sent Jim's spunk into the fire. James grunted, and he too shot out his spunk.

Their cocks were still hard. Neither of them pulled out, and the energy of the three men began to pick up again. Jim stood up straight, pulled Alejandro's cock out of his ass, turned and grabbed onto the kid's cock with his mouth. "A fucking horse dick," Jim thought, as it passed into his throat and then into his gullet. James pulled out of Alejandro and went to the back of Jim and stuck his cock into his man. He fucked him, fucked him hard. Jim always liked to know he was getting fucked; he liked it hard and fast. Filled from both ends, Jim was soon building up to thunder his guts out again.

Jim and James knew the drink was going to keep them there all night. Alejandro was ready for it.

The next morning at sunrise found Alejandro sleeping between the two men, with a cock in his ass and with his lips and tongue around another, a link between the two men. Before long, though, Jim and James saddled their horse and left for the city. Alejandro was already mounted on his horse and set off to the *rancheria* with a wave of his hat, although he probably wouldn't be wearing it for the next week or so.

Sweat and the dust of their travel from Los Angeles, as well as their firelight fuck, covered them. They were anxious to see Teddy before they soaked up a bath.

Teddy was an old friend, and the drifters knew he would be in the heart of the wildest place in town. Right in the middle of the Barbary Coast.

San Francisco was the newest, fastest, bustlingest little city west of the Mississippi, a sprawling, noisy place. Seen everywhere were people on horse, wagon, or foot. Ninety per cent of the people were men—sailors, ex-teamsters, ex-farmers, and a few ex-others, probably of more or less unlawful callings. Regardless of their past, they were all miners now, searching for that pot of gold. The sidewalks were full, and so were the hitching posts.

Jim reined in his horse at the corner of a building. Even though it was only several years old, the weathered boards made it look very much older. It was a disreputable looking place with a sign over the door: "Teddy's Emporium and Saloon."

This would turn out to be their favorite place in all of San Francisco, even though they had never been there before. If it was Teddy's place, then for the two men, there was no other.

They hitched their horses to the corner post and walked into the rear of the place. Sure enough, there he sat, running the whole show with a stogie in his mouth and a handful of cards in his fist. Behind him and to the side was a gigantic man dressed to kill. Dapper clothes and a shiny revolver let them know that this dude meant business.

Teddy looked up from his card game and yelled, "Eeoow! It's the two Jim's!"

Teddy threw his cards in the air, jumped up, and grabbed

both of them. The guy dressed to kill must have been day-dreaming because he had his pistol half-drawn. He quickly put it back. He was quick, but he would have to pay attention if he was to live very long—as a hired gun, that is. Teddy introduced them to Bear. It wasn't his real name, but Teddy had made it stick.

"When did you get in?" Teddy asked. "Just now, by the looks of it." He motioned to the table. "Sit down."

With a huge smile caused by the sight of his two buddies, he ordered Bear to fetch them both boilermakers.

"Well, how's the loves of my life?"

Teddy always received them the same way, with hugs and kisses and open arms. He loved them both, and on quite a few occasions had made plenty of room for them in his bed. This was Teddy.

Teddy was also the star performer at his place. He really knew how to sucker the pay dirt out of these miners. The only ones to miss Teddy's attention were the occasional drunks at the end of the bar. Teddy was very serious about his role as a man when he was wearing the clothes of a man.

On the other hand, he was an inveterate actress when he led off the night's activities adorned in a long dress. He was very much the person of his dress, whether it was the rough cotton of the pioneers or the soft silks he kept in his trunks. Even with his slight beard, he was a beautiful woman. And in his pants, he was a regular *caballero*.

His shows brought in more pay dirt than a gold mine. Nothing was cheap here except Teddy. His favorite opening song for the show was: "What Was Your Name in the States?"

That got everybody off on the right start. Nobody really cared about who you had been. Out here in this lawless country, it only counted who you were today.

"Hey, you buttfuckers, where ya been, out in the gold fields?" Teddy asked.

"Yeah," James replied.

"We thought maybe Southern California had a few undiscovered fields," he continued, "but I suppose we were wrong."

"You smelly old cunt! How're you hangin', or is it standin' again?" Jim asked.

"Shit, you two always get it to stand. It's good to see you. It's been duller 'n hell since I saw you last in Santa Fe. If it weren't for Bear hangin' around, I would have died without the two of you. He don't have two good cocks to shove in me like you two, but he's got enough in one to keep me from complaining." Teddy sighed. "People comin' and goin' to the fields are gettin' to me, even though they leave most of their pay dirt here. But then they're gone again. Incidentally, the vigilantes are at it again. It ain't been peaceful since those fellows in Monterey brought us all back into the States again. There's no place to go anymore, seems like."

As Teddy rattled on, it was clear that he was ready to move again. The two had heard this conversation before.

"Santa Fe, most probably," they said to one another with a glance.

"Now, if I could find two fellas like you around, and Bear, too, maybe it wouldn't be so bad to stick around San Francisco."

"Sorry to disappoint you, Teddy," said Jim, "but we're on our way to Sonora."

"Well, I guess I can handle it with Bear. Meantime this town's not so bad. This little gold mine will keep me happy. And then when I'm old and gray like Jim there, it'll keep me in men the likes of you, James."

With that crack, Teddy started laughing so hard he choked. Teddy always enjoyed himself. He would have gone on laughing for half an hour, if Jim hadn't interrupted him.

"Hey, when is the show starting? James and I want to go get cleaned up and take a little nap. We wanta get back in time to see you make an ass out of yourself in front of these dumb asshole miners," he explained with a wink.

"You got lotsa time," replied Teddy. "The first show is at seven o'clock tonight. And listen, there's a good bathhouse over on Market Street, at the bottom of Nob Hill. It's got lots of hot water and the hoity-toities from off the hill even stop in sometimes. One room even has copper tubs. I use that room all the time. They've also got a laundry there. When you're finished, drop by, and you two can take a nap in my room upstairs. I'd send Bear up with you," he said with a sideways glance at both of them, "but he has to watch over the day's receipts."

"Sounds great," James said as he got up. "Let's go, Jim. See you later, cunt!"

Jim smiled at the repartee and ducked under the glass that went flying by James' head. It crashed on the floor and came to rest next to a steady customer lying at the end of the bar. Teddy was known far and wide for his hospitality.

Almost every Swedish bath they had run across had a woman named Olga or a man named Ole running it. "Inga's Place" was a nice change. The large, heavy lady took good care of the two drifters. She saw a lot of drifters and treated them all like her sons, even those older than herself. Inga gave them each a towel, took their laundry, and showed them to a room with a copper tub, and then went on about her business. As they began hanging their clothes on the wall hangers, a handsome dude walked into the room and sat down. He had come from the steam room and was oozing with sweat. Wearing only a towel around his waist, he spread his legs and let his cock hang off the bench. The dude had a lot going for him. He had a monster hanging there. His hand lay on his thigh, his fingers flashing gold and diamonds.

James noticed something in the man's eyes as soon as he entered. The man was looking directly at him. James had noticed the look before in other men. Lust was certainly there, and sensuality, but there was something else. A madness was present, a private hell. It made James suddenly sad for the man: He was trouble.

The dude didn't see Jim at all, or so it seemed. He was a dark man, a bit swarthy. "Good eatin'" hung over his hips, not a lot but enough to be noticed. Completely disregarding the presence of Jim, the man crossed over to where James was taking off his pants. The man was standing in front of James now, and he reached out and grabbed James' cock.

James was fascinated by the man. He definitely was attracted to the physicality of the man, but the eyes didn't lie. James wanted no part of this man. He knocked the man's hand away assuredly, but with no malice. The dude was not happy about it. He knew that James was excited. He had seen it in James' first glance, first, right into his eyes, then down to his hanging cock. Twice, James' eyes had lingered more than long enough to see every inch hanging there.

In the meantime, Jim had stepped away to watch this exchange. When he saw James knock the hand away, Jim sat down. He knew this was going to be good, an exchange of favors.

"Hey, fella—watch who you're hittin'!"

The dude wasn't angry at his hand being knocked away—he was looking for a fight.

The dude grabbed James' shoulder and began to spin him around with James' ass facing the bulging towel. James swung his left fist as he was turning. The man was fast and had expected James to fight back, so he ducked the blow easily. He then tripped James and brought him to the floor.

Jim had seen James wrestling men before, but not with such vigor. Jim laughed at the two men wrestling about the floor. James had never fought with men much. He could take care of himself most times, but he would much rather love men than fight them. Before long, James was getting bested by the swarthy man. Jim knew James well enough to know that James had a good reason for not letting the man take his ass. Already, Jim had seen enough of the dude to agree with James' judgment.

By this time, the dude's towel had fallen away. The nude bodies of the men shimmered from the sweat of the struggle. The dude's cock had enlarged tremendously and had grown stiff. James' cock was stiffening too. It was the strength, the smell, and the physicality of the man that stiffened James' cock, but the evil in his eyes stiffened James' resistance. The man's weight was against James, who had been surprised and had never gained an advantage over the man. The big cock was about ready to enter James' ass when Jim stood up, picked up the stool he was sitting on, and bashed the man over the head. James pulled himself out from under the dude.

"You fuckin' cocksucker!" he barked at his partner. "It sure took you long enough. What took you so long? That bugger almost stuck me in the ass!"

"I wanted to see the bugger give you a good fuck. God knows you haven't had one for a damned long time."

Jim had enjoyed the whole incident and his infectious smile made James laugh. They both undressed and took their baths.

Jim got into the tub, and James joined him.

"I knew you couldn't handle yourself in the big city," Jim told him. "Good thing you asked me to come along." He laughed again, a great hearty laugh.

When they had washed the grime out of their pores and finished their bath, they dressed in their best clothes for Teddy's show. Before they left, though, they went over, picked the man up, and set him in the tub of dirty water. He was still out cold. He had a large lump on his head, but was breathing all right.

"Well, he's not dead," Jim said. "But when he comes to with a headache, he'll sure wish he was. Why do you suppose he got so rough with you? He's good enough to make men fight for him, not against him."

James looked at Jim. "This man is mean. He looks good until you really look into his eyes, and then you see it. It took me a few moments to see it. It was hard to get my eyes past his cock, but he is a dangerous man. C'mon, let's get outta here. I hope we never see that one again."

When they left, they told Inga that a drunk had passed out back in the tub. Poor Inga, all that laundry to heft about, and now she would have to take care of a drunk. Jim left her a big tip and said they would be back in a few days for the laundry. Then they headed back to Teddy's.

After the show, the three of them sat at Teddy's rear table and talked about the "good times," as Teddy called them.

"It's time to move on," she was saying (for she was still wearing her dress from the show). "I just don't know where to go. I've already been there."

She had a story about every city in the United States. Most of them, they had heard more than twice, but the stories were always good. You knew they were true because she never varied them, not one iota. And of course the two men had been with her for a few of the stories. It was good to see her.

"Hey! You two have heard all this." Teddy changed the subject. "What are ya up to these days, cocksuckers?"

"We're on our way to Sonora, in the Sierras just out of Fresno. 'There's gold in them there hills', like they say." James had seen that in an Eastern paper at the newsstand near Inga's. He laughed.

The lights in Teddy's eyes were sparkling. "Sonora, huh? I've never hit a small town. I wonder what it's like."

Teddy didn't like the looks of this little hick town. It wasn't a town; it was ruts, tents, and an occasional tent-and-board building.

"It's muddy, busy, and ugly," Teddy muttered to himself as he rode into the town. He and Bear were riding ahead of the wagon carrying his "boys."

"How can a man wear a dress in this town with all that mud?" Teddy muttered to himself. He was not pleased with his decision to leave San Francisco. "Bear, where is that saloon those two built for me?"

When there was no reply, Teddy looked around again. "Damn! What an ugly town."

It *was* an ugly town.

Teddy felt better about his decision, though, when he looked up and saw the two-story log cabin topped with a huge sign: "Teddy's New Emporium and Saloon."

The two Jims had done a good job. "Where are they?" he thought to himself as he stepped into the office. It was just like the one he had had in San Francisco—and then he realized that most of the furnishings had been carted from "Teddy's" in San Francisco.

It had taken a lot of gold dust to get all that stuff to San Francisco, and lots more to get it to Sonora.

Trustworthy men were hard to come by. All the ex-sailors and ex-teamsters and others were all miners now and just weren't available. James knew how to pick good men, though. He'd look them right in the eyes and know if they were worth their salt. Well, here it was April, and the two had done a good job in only six weeks, only where had they come up with the lumber? "Where are they now, the bastards?" Teddy wondered to himself.

"Are you Senor Teddy, or is it Senorita Teddy?" Alejandro said with a smile as he came down the stairs. "Excuse me, my name is Alejandro. Jim and James asked me to welcome you. They left two days ago and left me here to wait for you. They couldn't wait—they're at the mine."

"Just call me Teddy, buster," Teddy growled. "This guy is a real smart ass," he added to no one in particular. "What mine?" he continued, turning back to Alejandro. "What's going on around here? Who is running this place for me? Where are those bastards? They know I need them."

Alejandro realized he would have to unruffle Teddy's feathers.

"Senor Teddy, wait, now wait. I'm in charge. We have a grand opening the day after tomorrow. Jim and James finished the saloon a week ago, so they opened the doors a little early. They didn't think you'd want it just to sit here. James got into a poker game the first night and won a gold mine. I met them here the next day, after I lost my job on a *rancheria*, so they had me take it over till you got here. Everything is fine."

Teddy looked around. Alejandro seemed to have everything going smoothly, and his manner assured Teddy that everything was under control.

"We'll see," Teddy replied "But first, where is this mine?"

Just then, Bear walked in. Teddy gestured to him.

"Come here and listen to this. Now, Alejandro, where is this mine?"

Alejandro told them where the mine was and how to get there and was about to go into more detail when Teddy stopped him.

"Bear, you go get them and bring them back here. And don't take your time about it," Teddy ordered. "I know how you can hang out."

James was putting the day's sluicing in a poke when he heard a horse coming down the trail. The poke already had enough in it to buy all of San Francisco, he thought.

They had only been at the site a few days, and James knew he was exaggerating the truth a bit, but he was feeling real good about the work there at the mine. It was a good place, but who knew when the gravel beds would run out of the little gold flecks?

During the card game that had won the mine, he had drawn some pretty good cards, had done a good bit of bluffin', and some sweatin' too. Now all they had to do was work the claim.

Jim's back was killing him. His hands were blistered. Owning a gold mine was not as exciting as he'd always thought it would be.

James stepped out of the lean-to and looked up the trail.

"Well, I suppose Teddy is having conniptions. Here comes Bear."

"Hiya, Bear. How ya hangin'?"

Jim held Bear's horse as he climbed out of the saddle. Bear looked as good as ever, and in his riding clothes, a lot more rugged than he did in his dude clothes. He was still dressed to kill, his guns low-slung, but he had that smile and a twinkle in his eye. Bear was a good man. He had a great affection for life and a zest for fun that belied the deadliness of his guns.

While putting "Teddy's New Emporium and Saloon" together, Jim and James had run into some good men. Most had gone to the gold fields, but the two men they liked best were gonna stick around. Alejandro and Bear were good men. Alejandro had been run off the *rancheria* by the Don after he heard about the *gringos* on his land. Tough luck for the Don. Alejandro was worth his weight in gold. Even though he was a small man, he carried himself like a six-footer.

Bear had been good for them, too. A body felt safe with him around—at least, when he paid attention. He was an honest man and could pull rabbits out of his hat. The teamsters he had gathered together kept their word and brought in the wagons loaded down with Teddy's furnishings.

James had said to Jim several times, "Couldn't ask any more of a man to ride the trail with. Teddy's lucky to have Bear around."

James liked Bear. He seemed to be devoted to Teddy. It

didn't make sense, what with the way Teddy was always hanging off a man's arm like he did. But Teddy had set him straight on that score. Teddy liked to watch the big man get fucked. Teddy got off on it. Every night, he would bring a miner up the stairs who would be aching to get that cock of his up that dress of Teddy's and instead, would wind up fucking Bear. James and Jim had grinned and winked at each other, thinking about how the miners' faces must have changed when they got a look at Bear.

"Welcome to our mine, Bear," James said to the man, but he was wondering if Teddy was happy with the saloon they had built.

"Howdy," Bear said as he settled on the ground next to James. "Teddy sent me to get you all." He reached out his hand to James. "He wasn't as upset as he put on, so y'all don't have to hurry none. Where's Jim?"

James shook the hand and said, "He's out rustling up some fresh meat. He'll be happy to see the Bear meat when he gets back. Both of us have been hankerin' for Bear meat for about a month and a half now. The both of us have been too busy to get it, though—huh, buddy?"

"Yeah! Well, maybe we can take care of that little problem. It's too late to head back for Sonora today anyway."

Bear had started late for this very reason. He had been hot for the two Jims from that first day back in San Francisco when Teddy's yell had brought him out of his daydreams. Actually, though, he hadn't been daydreaming but only reliving the events of the night before. His ass had been plugged real good with an English sailor Teddy had brought upstairs. And right now, getting his ass plugged was foremost in his mind.

Jim called out from the ridge above the camp. "Howdy! Well, I'll be a son of a bitch!" Jim came into the camp, dropped the rabbit next to the fire, and hugged the big man. "Teddy sent you after us—right?"

James joined the two and stuck his tongue into the mouths of Bear and Jim. He loved it like this. His man, and one of the brothers, locked in physical embrace and loving one another. James pulled his tongue from the two.

"C'mon, let's cook this rabbit and eat. Then we can get down to some good loving."

The meal was good. The rabbit, mixed with the miner's lettuce that grew everywhere in the hills of California, and the herbs and mushrooms that sprouted up here and there, all mixed together and fried in the skillet over coals, made a great miner's meal. Coffee afterward, with a liberal sprinkling of the red mushrooms, made dessert.

The moon came over the ridge, rich and full. The light of the moon cast its shadow from the tall pines across the campsite. The fire had died to coals, so Jim put some more wood on it. The spring night was warm and held the heat of the fire in a radiant circle.

Bear stood up and began to peel off the clothes from his big frame. His cock wasn't as big as one would expect on a Bear. It was diminished in size only because of the size of the big man's body—a perfect symmetry of narrow waist, barrel chest, thick arms, and legs that were overpowering in the thickness of muscles strung from his ass to his heels.

The three of them were soon naked, their cocks shining in the flickering firelight under the shimmering moon. Bear bent over and sucked in James' cock and eased his ass toward Jim. Jim's cock pushed right in. Bear grunted and backed up, almost pulling off James' cock. James just pushed forward and started facefucking the big man.

Meanwhile, Jim had pushed in to the hilt and started fucking the man hard and fast. His asshole was big and deep, but the muscle control of Bear was very well trained. Jim could feel the muscle around his cock tighten and loosen and push and pull on his cock. Jim stopped fucking the man, pushed deep in, and remained there while Bear stroked the deeply buried cock with his ass muscles.

"God, this man is great!" Jim announced to no one in particular.

Jim looked down at the man simultaneously impaled on both his own cock and his lover's cock. Bear was loving every inch and every second of the fuck with the two men. The big man was gonna teach Jim something about taking a fuck in the ass, and Jim was gonna be a willing pupil.

James had had many mouths on his cock before. Some of them compared with Bear's, but none of them had been connected to the build or the classic good looks or the body of this man. He was a fuck-and-suck man all the way. He had been born to love men. The sole purpose of his existence was the enjoyment of sex—sex with men. These thoughts went through James' mind as he looked on the creature of God's love. James' balls were aching from the man's enveloping mouth and deep throat. He looked across Bear's back and into the eyes of his man, reached over the humping Bear, and opened his mouth for his lover's tongue. The moment was superb.

"Teddy's gonna be pissed he didn't see this," James said out loud to his two partners.

Bear, at this statement, began coughing, backed off the cock in his ass and the cock in his mouth, and started laughing. It took him a moment before he could reply.

"Well, he can't have everything." He was still laughing.

Jim and James were carried away by this man's laughter and joined him. They were having a wonderful time. After they stopped laughing, they finished things off.

The next morning took them back to Sonora.

"How much do you want for that mine?" Teddy didn't even say, "Hi!" before he got straight to the point. "I'll buy it from you. Damn, I need good men around me, and I don't need them traipsin' off all over the hills."

Jim laughed and asked Teddy, "Around you or in you?"

"Now stop that," Teddy said. "I'm serious. I got a place to run here and I gotta get this pay dirt to the bank. Whatta you want for that mine?"

Jim smiled at Teddy. Both he and James had discussed it before they had come into town. The gravel beds at their mine were fairly well cleaned out by the previous owner, and there was very little left, if any at all.

"Actually, we need a good job. The mine has petered out, and James and I weren't made to use a pick and shovel. We had a good poke out of it, but now we're ready to get on with something else. We'll take it—the job, that is. You still want to buy that mine?"

"I gotta get the show ready for the Grand Opening," Teddy said. "I've hired Alejandro to keep the place going, and you two are taking my loot to the banks in San Francisco, ya hear?" Teddy was pissed. He knew why they had been a day late. "The least you sons-a-bitches could have done was to wait for me."

They all knew Teddy would get over it.

"I'll bet it was great, wasn't it?" Teddy winked at the men. "Bastard buttfuckers."

Teddy went to his dressing room behind the stage.

"Well, what the hell do I care now, I have all of them to play with." Teddy laughed to himself. "And Alejandro, too."

He hadn't told his old friend all the facts of the matter. He hadn't been lonely, either. Alejandro was more than he could have asked for, though no more than Teddy could take.

Teddy finished the late show of the evening. It was good. She had brought a few of her boys with her from San Francisco, great little troupers. And the miners had been starved for entertainment, for Teddy and her boys were the closest thing to a woman most of them had known for some time. Circumstances had forced them all to share their beds with one another, and as one thing could, one thing led to another. Most of the miners preferred women, but would take a man or a boy before they would take a horse or a mule.

Teddy's show was always a hit. All she had to do was just stand there in a dress, and most of the men would be satisfied. But Teddy was a trouper. She always gave her customers a good show, more than enough entertainment to cover the cost of a poke.

Teddy sat in his office chair. At the table were James, Jim, Bear, and Alejandro, who were now all part of the inner circle.

"Jim, you and James are going to San Francisco next Wednesday. I expect to have a very large deposit," Teddy smiled. "This little place is going to buy me Nob Hill. You wait and see."

It looked good for all of them: James and Jim to guard the pay dirt, Alejandro to guard the saloon, and Bear to guard Teddy.

Jim and James arrived in San Francisco late the next Thursday afternoon. It had been a long trail from Sonora. Teddy didn't trust any bank shipments with the highway robbers around. He wanted it deposited directly in the San Francisco banks. And, he figured, "Who better to do it than a couple of ex-highway robbers?"

The two men made an early start and went the long way to avoid the major trails into the city. They had already made it to the bank and made the deposit. Soon, they were saying hello to Inga, when the dark swarthy man of their previous visit, the one Jim had cold-cocked, walked in off the street. He recognized both Jim and James, quickly turned on his heels, and strode out the door without looking back.

Inga said, "That man's very angry with you two." She smiled, remembering the appearance of the dude in the tub when she went in to clean the room after the two had left the last time. Then very seriously she added, "He's very powerful, very rich. I don't like the man, but he pays me well. He knows I could ruin him on the Hill for what he does here, but I don't care what he does here. Men are men, and that's the way they like it here. I love them for it. He and his friends could close me down, so I try to be nice to them. They're on the Vigilante Committee, and have made it very tough on plenty of people in town."

Jim pinched Inga on the cheek and said, "Thanks for the warning, but don't worry—we can take care of it."

Jim winked at James as they headed for the bathroom.

Later, they decided to go to the Barbary Coast. Their work was finished for the time being. They were cleaned up and in the wildest little town west of the Mississippi. They were ready for the love of Saint Francis. The two men crossed Market and into an alley to cross over to Mission Street. It was a dark alley, and halfway through it, they saw the swarthy man with a companion, their pistols drawn. Before Jim and James could think, they heard footsteps behind them. They were in trouble.

The swarthy man said, "I've been checking you two out, and now you're gonna pay for what you did to me"

Jim's head exploded, and before James knew it, three men had pinned him to the wall of the alley. The dude was whispering in his ear. "You're gonna die for it. He's gonna live for it. Live without you for what he did to my head."

He put the rope around James' neck and pulled it tight, choking off his yell.

Jim returned to San Francisco in July of 1858. His voyage had been long. Two years ago, no telling how long after that night in the alley, he had awakened in the hold of a ship. The ship's master was standing over his wet body with an empty pail in his hand. His clothes had been taken from him and he was chained to the hull. His head ached. He looked around for James but didn't see him.

The ship's master said, "So yer gonna be a miner, huh? Well, sailor, it's gonna be a long while before you see the gold fields again. We're on our way to Shanghai." The man laughed.

It had been a tough two years not knowing what happened to James. Now he knew. He had found out the other day. Teddy had told him what happened.

"The VC got James," Teddy had said.

And today Jim stood in front of the new marble tombstone. "The bastards. . .Oh, God. . .James. . ." ▼

❖ ❖ ❖ ❖ ❖ ❖ ❖

THE
RITUAL

❖ ❖ ❖ ❖ ❖ ❖ ❖

The Ritual

❖ ❖ ❖ ❖ ❖

There he is again. That's three times this week. He doesn't see me yet. Is he going to look away again?

The first time I saw him was on the boardwalk at Fire Island this last summer. He had just come out of the dunes. He was wearing a Speedo-type suit that was really tight on his hard cock. It just sort of bounced with his every step. I was a good long way from him and walking toward him. It seemed we were moving in slow motion. His cock bobbed and seemed huge, even at the distance I was from him.

As I got closer, I saw that it wasn't just the late afternoon shadows, it wasn't a quirky fold in his suit, it wasn't my over-active imagination—it was huge. It's a good thing I looked up and into his face or I never would have been able to recognize him later on. He had reddish-blond hair, long but not hippie, a mod style. It was mussed from the sun, wind, and salt water. He had the blue eyes that you only see once in awhile. Classic face, not a model's, but rugged. He had a trim beard and looked like a red-haired Morgan the Pirate. His chest was heaving from walking across the sands of the dunes. Heavy chest, thighs, and calves. He stopped and stomped the sand from his feet right in front of me. I got to see the cock twitch as it bounced from the stomping feet. He looked directly into my eyes.

No way, no way. This isn't going to be the man to kill me with his diseases. Yet, if you want to talk about a man to die for, this one was it.

He sort of sidestepped as he stomped and put himself almost into my path. The boardwalk was narrow at that point where it falls into the little dune forest, and so I had all I could do to stay on the walk as I passed him. He thrust his pelvis forward and brushed my arm with his cock. It was cock. I could feel it. The cloth had pulled away from his stomach from the pressure of his cock. I looked down as I passed. The cockhead was not only peeking out of the cloth but also out of his foreskin. I saw the pisshole and could swear that it pulsed open with a heartbeat. Like I said, this was all in slow motion. I speeded up the action by moving on.

I am not going to give my life away for a few seconds in the dune forest.

I walked on, just a bit stiff-legged. I looked down, and there it was, thrusting its head downward out of my Bermuda shorts. Even these long shorts could never hide my aroused being. Before the epidemic, I had teased my way through half of New York with my "El Grand." That's past—never could I be that kind of whore again.

"God, my cock aches." I veered off the boardwalk to a path that went deep into the bushes. "God I can't handle this," I groaned.

As the path dwindled to a little hole in the bushes, I pulled out my cock. Both hands pulling on it had made the head ooze, so it began to slip more easily out of the foreskin. It didn't take more than a few strokes. I grunted as I came. Not that jerkoff is boring to me, but it had been a long time since I had been with anyone. I'd long ago stopped calling my buddies. John, my best buddy, I can't call anymore. I'd even changed my phone number, and now I don't give it out, period. I wonder why I keep it.

"It's not gonna happen to me," I said as I wiped my dick with my hand.

You can't live and be sexual these days. I have lost too many friends. All of my buddies are gone, even John. They're all on the other side. My dreams and nightmares. I see them at night beckoning. John, like captain Ahab riding the back of Moby Dick with his lashed body and his arm beckoning to his crew to follow, comes through the space of my dreams, beckoning and giving me his summons:

"Follow me. Come, come with us."

No. I am not going to follow. I won't go.

I saw this fellow next on Christopher Street. He was coming out of the subway, right after me. I was on my way to Ty's and had stopped to look at a magazine, *Honcho* or *Stallion*, something for my safe sex play at home. I was horny again. I was depressed. Even worse, I had been cockteasing again. Just standing on street corners, next to walls, pushing that bound cock of mine into the air space in front of my hips. Before I'd gone out, I'd bound my cock with the leather strap I had brought at "Mister S" in San Francisco. None of the leather shops in Manhattan could make me a strap eight feet long. I needed the length to properly bind my balls and cock. (The most I could get in Manhattan was four feet.) "Mister S" takes the strap out of the middle of the hide. It wastes a bit of leather, but because of the way they make their chaps, it works. I had done a little leather work, so I knew the problem. Rawhide thongs cut too deeply to wear for long periods of time. For my purposes, it had to be a long strap.

Here's what I do: I take my balls in my left hand and stretch them out. With my right hand, I start a clockwise turn of the strap around the base of the ball-sac, and with concentric circles, move the strap out to the end. That stretches my balls to the tightest, making a big ball on the end of a leather-sheathed shaft. I always use at least five feet of strap for this. Then I cross over the top of my cock and then around the cock at the base. Grabbing my cock and my balls with my left hand, I stretch out my cock and balls and continue the strap around my bound cock and balls and over the short-cut pubic hairs till my cock seems even longer than it really is. I take the loose end of the strap and tuck it under at the base of cock, balls, and strap.

By this time my cock is hard, and there is no way it will go down until it's unstrapped. I pull my Levi's on, being careful not to grab myself in the V-crotch as I tug the denim over my thigh. My balls go out over the right side of the V-crotch. I button the top button of my Levi's and reach down and carefully stuff my balls into my right pant leg. Then I grab the hardened cock and push and stuff it into the same leg as the balls. I grab my vest off the clothes tree with my chaps. The vest covers my pierced tits. It's difficult to bend over with the strapped cock and balls in my pants leg stiffening my body movements. I zip the legs up, and the leather snugs under my cock and balls, pulling the Levi's at least an inch or two out and over the top of the chaps.

I didn't use to pricktease. I'd do myself into this leather image, go out on the town, and come home with the hottest dudes. Now I just cocktease and come home and put that strapped cock into my hand and blow it off.

My cock had been stuffed into the Levi's for two hours on that particular day, and was really straining the strap, the denim, the chaps, and my mind. I was walking quickly to my "digs" in Loisaida, otherwise know as the Lower East Side. I was hot to blow it off.

He saw me before I saw him, or so I thought at the time. Actually, he told me later, he had been following me for two hours at a discreet distance, enjoying the reactions to my teasings. I walked into him again while leaving the newsstand. We bumped, then I looked up and into his face and suddenly recognized who it was. Right there on the street, he grabbed my strapped cock and let out a little whistle under his breath that only I could hear. I pulled away.

This guy is gonna bust my balls. Now I have even more reason to hurry. Prickteasing gets me horny all right, but I have to go home alone. God it's been a hell of a three months. Is that all—just three months? Ah shit. I can't go on like this. It's hell. And now, today, here he is again.

He walked directly to me and put his arm on the wall. I couldn't go around him. The trash cans on the left, the double-parked and bumper-to-bumper traffic made the street a mess. His arm covered the right. I could turn around and go the other way, but his voice stopped me.

"What's it gonna be? Am I gonna have to wrestle you to the ground? Am I gonna have to knock you on your kiester and carry you home on my shoulder and then rape you? No matter what, you're mine. And you're mine today, ya fucking cocktease."

I could have turned, but I didn't. I said, "Three months ago you coulda had me easy. Today, a snowball in hell would have a better chance of freezing than you've got of getting in my pants, buddy."

"What's the matter with you? You tell me in every way you want me and my cock to show you a good time. Shut up and let's get outta here."

He doesn't know that I'm a carrier. I'm just a Typhoid Mary cruising around and killing my guys. I know it. John is gone. Jerry, Michael, they are all gone. All my buddies. I'm just not going to do it again. I turn and begin walking down the street. The guy runs and catches up to me. He grabs my arms and yanks me around to look at him.

"I've been after your ass for over three months, fella. You

don't think you ran into me by accident do you? John sent for me. He sent for me for you. He knew you would need a big hole with him gone. He knew you needed a big one for your hole. He gave me a letter for you. I thought you'd be ready long before this. You're sure hard to pin down. You were supposed to come of your own free will, but I can't go on setting this up over and over again. You can only pricktease so long before it's too late. You either come with me now or I'll bring you. It's your choice."

He was big, but so am I. Still, I could see his determination. I'd seen it all this time. My resolve shattered. I let him lead me down a side street near Sheridan Square. *What a laugh—he lives on Gay Street*. He took me into one of those little Greenwich Village apartments where the kitchen, the closet, and the living room merge into a room the size of a California walk-in closet. The door opened outward into the hall. The floor was a wrestling mat, a wall-to-wall wrestling mat with pillows all over it. It smelled vaguely like a vanilla milk shake. He sat me on some pillows, walked over to the closet, and pulled out a briefcase. He handed me the letter. It was a thick manila envelope with a small white pamphlet that was titled *How to Have Sex in an Epidemic: One Approach*.

I read the letter:

> *Dear Randy,*
> *I gave this letter to my brother to give to you. I'll be gone when you read this letter. I hope I'm not forgotten. I have always loved you. I gave you the space, allowed you the space to be what you are. I know your street habits. I used to follow at discreet distances. I know how you love it.*
> *Just after I last saw you, I found this book at the Oscar Wilde book store. I bought it for you. I know you think you killed me—that you're a carrier. You told me that. I don't believe it. Who knows? It could have been anybody in New York. God knows I tried to get everybody. That doesn't matter, anyway. There are too*

many unknowns for anybody to blame anybody about this disease.
It's here, it's reality—who should know better than I?

Randy, it's not who we did, it's not what we did, it's not where
we did it, it's not when we did it, nor even why we did it. It's how
we did it. When I think of all the assholes we have rimmed, all the
cum we've ingested, it's no wonder. If it wasn't this plague, it
would have been another one. We were ripe for it. We set ourselves
up for it. When I read in the book that we eroticized our oppres-
sion, I had to nod my head in agreement. This book is right on. It
is how we did it, with complete abandon, without regard for our
health, with total irresponsibility. We didn't know better. There
was no one to tell us. Mother Nature played a dirty trick on us.
In trying to stop over-population, she gave us AIDS. How ironic
that she chose a manner that inadvertently caused the deaths of
those who are not populating the planet! At this point in my life,
the irony is wasted on me.

What this book tells us, though, is that AIDS and all sexually
transmitted diseases are preventable. It's a manual of how to do
it.

I have discussed the book with Joe—he was the one who recom-
mended it to me. It's too late for me, but not too late for you. Read
it, and have Joe answer your questions. Use your good common
sense. Rimming and the other things are no longer important.
What is important is that we love one another enough to stop shar-
ing our diseases, that we love one another enough to give ourselves
without killing one another. I love you, and I miss you.

John

I put the book down and looked up. John's brother, Joe,
had slipped out of his clothes and was standing in front of me.
His V-chest was trimmed. The hair all over his body was cut
to about an eighth of an inch, including his pubic hairs and
armpits. He reached out and pulled me up. His cock standing in front of him stuck into my hip and pushed.

"Come here, Randy. The ritual is about to begin."

He pulled me into the bathroom and brought out a pair of hair clippers. He started on my legs and began to peel the hair from my body. Joe was quick with the clippers. He cut a swath across my crotch, then slid the clippers down the shaft of my cock and into the thick bush. The hair fell off the clippers and began to make a pile of the tiled floor. Next, he ran the clippers around my ass and up deep into the crotch. The shearing head tickled and made goose bumps all over, making the hair stand out from the body, and making the clipping much easier. It was a thrill feeling the head move around my body. Shivers went up my spine to the back of my head and exploded into my brain. My cock throbbed with my heart as the clippers finished the job. Joe looked at my face. My beard and my hair. He cut another swath across each side of my head leaving only about a half-inch of hair above my ears. He went down under my throat and up over my cheeks. I could see him in the mirror running the clippers around my body, getting those last little hairs that he missed in the first strokes. He looked good. Every time he moved, his hard cock throbbed to the buzz of the clippers. He grabbed my cock and the clippers in both hands, as the motor throbbed against my cock like a vibrator. He smiled into my face and then grabbed my ear lobes with his teeth. As he pulled away from me, he put the clippers in my hand.

"Your turn to do me."

I started with his feet, and although there was not a lot of hair to clip because it was so short, there was enough to make a little job of it. When I got to his head, I decided to give him a Mohawk. When he was done, we both stood in front of the mirror and looked at one another.

"You got a razor?"

"Not yet," he replied.

When we got in the shower, he pushed my back so that I bent over at the waist. He adjusted the temperature of the water and turned the valve so the water would flow into the hose. He pulled another length of hose from the linen closet and attached it to the first, then stuck it in my ass. I felt the water swirling and gushing up inside me. Joe stepped aside as I shot the water from my hole down the drain. It felt good filling up to the bursting point and then thrusting it out from deep inside my body. I swallowed the hose and water with my asshole. Each time, he stuck the hose in deeper and fuller to clean the inside of my body. Gawd, it felt good! Washing and rinsing lasted for what seemed hours. Finally, he stopped, reached into the closet, and brought out another hose to re-place my hose with his. He shoved it into my hand.

"Now me," he said.

He bent over, and I shoved the hose in. It sank deeper and deeper into his body. His ass squeezed and sucked on that hose. I didn't believe the amount of water he could hold in there. I stepped aside as the water began to pour out of his hole. It was a flood.

Finally, it was over, and my cock had not let up for a mo-ment. So far, we were an hour into the ritual and we had not even touched each other's cock, yet not for a moment had our cocks shriveled. They were harder now than at any other time. Joe stood up and reached for the loofah sponge in the caddie. He rinsed me and then grabbed a bottle of dark red stuff. It said "Betadine Solution" in green letters on the plastic bottle. He opened the dispenser head and began to soap up my body.

"This is what surgeons use to scrub up for operations. Now then, give me a scrub."

He handed me the loofa sponge, and the Betadine, and I began to scrub. Up till then, there was very little of John that I could see in Joe. Now, as I scrubbed his body, I could see John's body on him. John had dark hair, though, and Joe's body hair blended from blond chest hair to deep red pubic hairs, sprinkled liberally with white. Joe's years, besides the white body hair, could be seen in his eyes. Joe had been around awhile. Joe picked up a nail brush and liberally sprayed Betadine on my hands as he scrubbed my fingers.

"We'll have to do your nails first. Then mine."

We stepped out of the shower and into a heavy duty, electric, wall hand-dryer. His was mounted above our heads. No towels.

Jon handed me a glass with hydrogen peroxide to gargle with. He then led me to the mats.

What a beautiful cock! The head of his cock was taking a big peek out of the foreskin. I could see it better now that it was outside the Speedo. In fact, my face was exactly two inches from the pulsing head. The pisshole did open and close with his heartbeat; his whole cock did throb with his heartbeat. Before I could suck it in, Joe pulled away and silently grabbed a little blue cartridge, pulled out a sheath, and stretched it over his fat cock. The end with the rubber band on it only reached halfway down his cock; it was that big. Then, on his knees, he shoved that cock into my throat. Deeply. It was elbow level and I felt the cock spear down into my body. The latex tasted terrible, but I didn't gag. I only gag myself when I want the waves of muscle response to milk a man's spasms of cum deep into my throat. Guys would panic when I did that to them. They'd pull off and ask if I was okay. I'd just jump right back onto the fucker and gag some more. Joe pulled out and spun me around. He began to slap my ass with his open hand—first one side, then the other. He picked up the tempo as well as slapping harder and harder.

It's wonderful. I love it.

He slowed down the tempo, then stopped, reached out, and spread my ass with both hands. I spread my legs wider to give him a little help. With one hand gripping my ass, he began to slap my hole. Again, he began picking up the tempo. He was getting savage with me, and all I could do was to take it and want more. My hole puckered and my cock bobbed with every slap. I looked under to see my cock throbbing with each slap and each pull of my sphincter. He slowed the tempo and stopped.

Reaching over to a shelf, he grabbed a grease gun. He opened a canister of creamy white lubricant. The smell of vanilla that had been wafting around the apartment suddenly grew stronger. He sucked the cream into the gun and screwed the top on, then reached to pick up a short length of hose and stick it onto the end of the gun. Slowly, methodically, he spread a thick layer of cream around the hose and knelt behind my ass.

While he was filling the gun, I hadn't moved. I looked at his movements and thought he was very graceful for a man his size. I opened and closed my hole like the iris of an eye or a camera adjusting to different shade of light and dark. It was pulsing in the slow tempo of the last slaps Joe had wielded. The odor of vanilla was stronger now.

Joe stuck one greased finger in my ass. I opened wide and barely felt it. If he were trying to open me up, it was too late. I was open. He pulled his finger out and shoved the hose in. I could feel the squeeze of his hand right through the gun. Each movement of his hand filled my hole a little bit more. It felt great to have the grease push in while I sucked it out.

Joe removed the gun from my ass. He pulled the hose off the end and squeezed some more grease into his hand. He grabbed his sheathed cock and slowly began to smear the grease the length and breadth of his rockhard erection. He placed his left hand on my back and pulled close to my butt. I felt the head of his cock go in.

Damn, do I love it.

I backed into him as he pushed forward. His balls met my ass, and I thought sure they were going to be pushed in along with his cock. My asslips started to suck, hoping that I could get those big balls in my ass along with his cock. Responding, Joe began to pick up the tempo again. He began to gallop his cock into my ass. I could feel the grease spitting out the sides and dripping down the side of my leg.

Gawd damn, he's good.

He shoved me forward just after I had reached under and grabbed my own cock. His plunges and my hand on my cock were hurtling me into the valley of orgasm. He shoved harder, and I fell to the mat. My face slid along the rough surface until my body was fully onto it, except for my ass which was pushed up into his cock. He shoved harder. I pushed back. I felt another inch of his cock come into me. He shoved again. I pushed again. Another half-inch. Jesus! He pulled out to the head and pushed forward with all his weight. My ass collapsed onto the mat. I got another half-inch into me.

Does he have more?

"Give it to me! Fuck me! Fuck my ass good!" I moaned.

Three months is much too long. I need this in my life. I can't live without cock.

My hand beneath my body felt every inward thrust of his cock filling my being. My cock engorged, pulsing to each thrust. He'd groan on the way in; I'd grunt on the way out. Grunt; groan. As the tempo speeded up, the sounds began to blend. Grunts and groans mingled to one great roar. We came together. My spurting cum began to make the mats slippery. My pelvis was sliding around. He came again. I came again. It seemed that this moment was here to stay.

Joe reached under me and pulled my body up. His hands were locked to my hips. My back arched as he thrust forward with his pelvis and back with his arms. He hit bottom with the head of his dick and spurted even more cum into the rubber. I shot again. Finally, he shoved me to the mat again, and we both collapsed, rolling onto our sides, gasping for breath. I felt his mouth at my ear.

"That's a good beginning," he whispered. ▼

SAFE
DEPOSIT

Safe
Deposit

❖ ❖ ❖ ❖ ❖

My nocturnal sex habits have changed. The hot sex clubs, the baths, and the streets have noticed my absence, but my throbbing cock notices it more. Hot and hungry for the release that's necessary for my life, I think sometimes I'll go mad. My cock's life is threatened. The monogamy that some people exist on can't give my cock the hardness or the power of the thrust that comes in the back rooms or the alleys where the confrontation is maximized by the anonymity of the receiver.

Tonight, though, I long for release. My cock is hungry. I have made up my mind: I'm going to do it. But I'm not going to be irresponsible about it.

The drug store is filled with Italian women greeting each other. ("Have a Happy Mother's Day.") Of course, the clerk would have to be a woman.

"Where may I find the prophylactics?" I ask.

"There on the wall," she points.

Pink, blue, and yellow boxes covered with minimal advertising, claiming comfortable love, are displayed on the wall. So many brands, some lubricated with something called nonoxynol-9, some dry. Decisions. Which should I buy?

I've never liked the idea of rubbers. Similar to dildoes, rubbers are impersonal. But then, isn't street sex impersonal, anyway?

The woman is looking at me as I make my selection. I'm nervous about the whole thing. At the same time, a curious feeling fills me. Excitement swells from my crotch. My cock is twitching in my pants. I refuse to look at her. The idea of rubbers becomes more appealing to me as I stand and look at them all arrayed in their colored boxes. I remember the last time I had the nerve to buy a condom. Condom, such a silly word. I was only about eighteen. I remember how excited I was then, too. I remember also that I really didn't enjoy "rubber sex." No feeling. Sort of lifeless, through the rubber, which would crawl, get bunched up, get folds in it. In those days, I only used it to jack off. I had no one to play with at that time. I was asexual, because I knew I didn't want a woman and was too scared to find a man. So my brief encounter with rubbers had convinced me that they weren't all that much fun.

Tonight, now, I finally decide on non-lubricated "Trojans." I might as well Greek with a Greek. The embarrassment over, I walk home with a growing bulge in my pants, as my cock grows in anticipation of feeling the cold night air turning into a sopping wet howl. I know the rubber will be too difficult to put on in the dark, so I decide to put it on just before leaving the house. I take a shower and grope my semi-hard cock. It won't go down—not that I want it to. A hardening cock always gives me a feeling of great power. I dress quickly, and before buttoning my pants, I stand in front of my dressing mirror and begin to pull on my cock. Cock, now that is a word to pick up and use, use it a lot.

I can't understand the hardness of my cock tonight, since I really didn't like my first experience with a rubber. Now my hard cock makes it easy to roll the rubber over the swollen head and down the shaft. The rubber ring slips all the way to where my balls snug up to my cock. With the ring tight around the circumference of my shaft, my cock gets even harder than before. I hope the rubber is strong enough to withstand it. I remember laughing to myself when I bought the damned thing. I wanted to ask the clerk if she had them in extra large. I'm glad I didn't.

Playing with my cock for another minute, I think I may shoot, and rather than ruin the evening, I begin to put it away, but before I do, I take another look at it in the mirror. The large vein running down the center of it pushes the rubber up and out from the shaft. The skin color at first has been very white, but as soon as the rubber adheres to the shaft, it becomes more flesh-colored. Its sensitivity is lessened, but my hand's touch through the insensitive rubber makes my mind reel. God damn, my cock gets even harder. The constrictive ring, as well as the tightness of the stretched rubber, is strange and new. I struggle to push the hardness into my pants and button up. The rubber-covered shaft brushing my leg feels good. Real good.

Many times, while walking around and doing the daily routine, I forget about my cock in my pants. With the rubber on, I become constantly aware of it. My mind is using the rubber as an aphrodisiac. The pressure of the tight Levi's rubs against the tight rubber. So far, I love it.

I get on the subway knowing that my crotch is heavy and showing a raging hard-on. Of course, the only ones who see it are the ones who are looking. All the looks I get are appreciative. I come out of the hole in the ground at Christopher Street. I head toward the river.

Since the health crisis, there's been a lot of cruising on the street, but no takers. I know I won't be getting anything off the street—everybody is running scared. Cautious. So how to do it is the problem. Well, I'll cross that bridge when I come to it. Meantime, I'm getting a lot of hungry looks. I stop about halfway to the pier and lean on a wall with my crotch out.

"How'm I going to find a buddy to stick it into?" I ask

myself. I have no answer.

My cock, with all the attention it's been getting both from me and the various people I have shown it to, is still getting harder. I set it to throbbing in my pants and make it twitch as a couple of guys walk by. One almost runs into a parking meter. I laugh a bit to myself. Here I am being a cocktease. I've always hated somebody to do that to me, but that's what makes exhibitionism: you're absolutely nothing without an audience. The pressure of the rubber is almost as hard as the pressure from the eyes. Here I am standing on the street with my cock twitching and nothing happening.

After about twenty minutes of me wanting it and other people wanting it, I give up my particular part of the wall and stroll down to the pier area. There I luck out. I meet John.

John is an old fuck buddy of mine who sort of drifted away. We begin talking. He never takes his eyes off my crotch. Finally he looks into my eyes and says, "Christ, I'm so horny for that cock of yours."

What he says comes as no surprise. I have known from the moment he spotted me that he wanted it again, always had, but because he knew I was a loner, he had drifted. Who knows why, who has the time to find out, who really cares?

Once or twice is always enough for me with most men. John, though, he was different. I remember John as being an expert cocksucker. He'd go wild sucking on the thickness and sucking it all the way to the balls while I'd whisper in his ear, "Cock, motherfucker. Cock. Cock. Suck it, suck cock. . .Cock. . .Cock. . .Suck it, buddy, suck that cock. Yeah, sucker, take it, take my cock all the way. Cock. Cock. . .Cock. . .Cock."

That always did it for him. I can remember how he had played with his own cock, and I can still hear him groaning and screaming, his mouth filled with cock, my cock. And the humming sound, loud, coming from his throat, vibrating my cock and balls and into my very body. I can remember how he'd come all over his hand and my shoes while his mouth was filled to the gullet with cock, how that muffled scream vibrating through my body got my sphincter muscle to working, how it would pump and push jism out of my prostate down my shaft and into his mouth.

Reflecting back on the job this John had once done on me, my cock is now throbbing once again. I can see how agitated he is becoming. He starts to say good-bye, but I stop him. I grab his arm and pull his hand into my crotch. He hesitates, but then he grabs real good and shoves his hand further into my crotch.

He looks into my eyes and says, "I'd love to, but I've changed my ways."

"I'm wearing a rubber," I say.

His eyes glisten at the news. "A rubber," he whispers. "A rubber? Let's go to my place. It's just around the corner."

I say, "Just suck on it, buddy. No kissing, okay?"

I sound like my fraternity buddy from college. It was always okay with him to suck my cock, but kissing was a little too queer for him. Well, things are different today: it's certainly not because I don't want to.

"Sounds good to me, Cocksman," John says as he turns and pulls me up the street with him.

I follow, almost stiff-legged because my cock is so bunched up in my Levi's and wanting to get out.

He turns around with his cock already in his hand. It is already hard. He drops to his knees and begins unbuttoning my pants. He really has to struggle to get my cock out. Finally, he just grabs the top of my Levi's and pulls. The buttons fall open like a zipper. My cock has broken free and is standing out, hard and beautiful. He just sits there, pulling on his own hard cock, looking and drooling.

"It's not going to be the same," he says, "but I don't care."

With that comment still on his lips, my cockhead becomes

even more engorged than at any time in my life. I'm sure the rubber is going to break at the head.

"God, what if it does?" I think.

But the rubber holds before it disappears down his throat, all at once, in one big gulp, until my balls are nestled against his chin. He wants it all.

It's strange. I know it's my cock in his throat, but I feel separated from my cock. The insensitivity is erotic. I have never used a rubber with anyone before, just with myself, and now I have this rubberized cock pulled into this man's throat. Is the scene going to be dull? Well, so far I'm not bored with the idea. I concentrate on the unfeeling rubber stretched over my cock, tightly enclosing it in a pressurized sheath of tightness. I imagine it to be the foreskin cut from my body when I was only minutes old, the foreskin I never experienced, the envy I have experienced over the years in my search for a real cock, not a butchered one.

"Is this what having a foreskin is like?" I ask myself.

I reach down and pull John up from the depths of his consciousness and grab his cock with one hand while I pull another rubber out of my pocket with my other hand. I roll the rubber down his hard shaft and push him to the floor. We plunge into each other, the rubberized dicks buried in each other's mouth.

The throbs and pulses are constrained by the pressure of the rubbers. My saliva lubricates the resistant rubber. The friction and new sensation on my throat are not yet a pleasant feeling, but not as unappetizing as I thought they would be. I taste the rubber. I'm really ready for this. I can see the condom on his shaft as it slides in and out of my mouth. I pull it out and look at it for some time. The rubber, like mine, adheres to every contour of his fine cock. I take the whole thing into my throat, all the way to the depths that his cock can reach. I want more.

I can feel, with my fingers in that area between his ass and his balls, the base of his cock pulsing, as the shaft gets harder and harder, and again I hear and feel that scream welling up from his balls. He is coming. The rubber in my mouth begins to balloon into my throat, and then I too am screaming a muffled cry of severe bliss back to him.

We pull apart, looking at each other's cock. Then we look at each other, sigh, and fall apart. I stand up and look down.

The bubble at the end of the rubber is filled with my jism. I work my cock some more with my hand. The rubber fills my hand. Back and forth, I stroke again and again. The jism wells up from within me, as the rubber slides back and forth over the head of my dick. I shoot another load. The rubber is now filled with a foamy white jizz and slips off easily.

I know John wants to suck on it, because I too want his used rubber in my mouth, sucking out the foam. But I drop the rubber in the waste basket, fall to the floor again, and give John a big hug.

"Not too bad," I say. "Not bad at all."

John just nestles into my arms and gives me a wink.

Like I said before, my nocturnal sex habits have changed. Yeah, I've changed a lot. So has John. I'm not the loner I used to be, and John likes it this way, too. Not that we still don't go out on the street. We're both sure about that. . .there is nothing like street sex. John loves those cocks, and me, I love those mouths.

It's been three years now that we've been stalkin' together. *We* figure, with the incubation period being over, and since we have been really playing it safe on the street, maybe one of these days we can get down to the real thing. He still has his place, I have mine. The streets are still ours, but his cum is mine and mine his. That's the way it is these days. ▼

❖ ❖ ❖ ❖ ❖ ❖

ALTAR
PIECE

❖ ❖ ❖ ❖ ❖ ❖

Altar
Piece

❖ ❖ ❖ ❖ ❖

My throat was dry, so I went up to the bar and ordered a beer. My first visit as a member, to the New York Jacks was already more than what I had thought it would be. So much cum all at once! Jerkoffs, they were all jerkoffs! The solitary act that is rumored to cause blindness or to make you grow hair on your palms, was here being performed by the Jacks in unabashed freedom. The cold beer felt good going down my throat. As I turned from the bar, I almost ran into one of the Jacks from the last circle jerk.

"Thanks, Richard. It's been one of my best sessions here."

He reached down and pulled his half-soft cock a stroke or two. "You really have made our night here. I saw your show at the Ramrod when you first came to New York. You sure are an inspiration. It's like having the King of Jerkoffs here. I just wanted to say thank you."

"A pleasure. I love to get compliments about my show. Thanks."

"Hot cocksman, that's what you are."

I looked around and there we were. The New York Jacks.

Some of us now taking a break were standing in groups talking, while those who were wrapped around their cocks were still going at it.

My cock started to get hard after the softness that had held since the last circle jerk. My cock was ready to go again. I was looking at a young blond man. He was tall and thinnish, but with nice musculature, a swimmer's body. His cock matched his body, long with thinnish musculature. He was standing on the side, just out of the light. A little light spilled off his shining chest, which was sweaty from the heat his hand had worked up. His eyes glittered in the darkness. He looked like a little boy in a toy store with a thousand dollars in his pockets. There was something about him—the attitude, the excitement—that was different from the other Jacks. I wandered over to a place close by him, but out of his eyesight. He was looking at a group of three men standing in front of a riser in the middle of the floor. As I watched, several more Jacks came up to the riser, a four-foot square, a little lower than waist height.

The blond man's cock was hard as any cock I have ever seen. His body was hard, too, every muscle held rigid by the pumping of his hand on his cock. He stepped closer to the group and was now in the light. The group of men around the riser saw him but made no move to allow or disallow him to join them. The group was one, yet all were intent for themselves. It's hard to explain their "oneness." The blond man wasn't an outsider—he was only outside because he hadn't joined.

I held back. I wanted to watch this man. Now that he was slightly in front of me, I got a good view of his ass. In a circle situation, all you usually see is cock. His cock was now hidden from my sight. I couldn't, but I wanted to walk up to his ass and put my hard cock into the rounded flesh squeezed tight by the muscles of his legs and back. The man was taut, all over taut. He stepped through the group to the riser, turning. He laid his body across the riser with his head hanging over the other edge. He looked up at the circle around him. I knew then why he had been so excited. He wanted the cum of all these men. The pig! He wanted the whole cupcake. Well, if he wanted it all, he'd have to have mine as well. I stepped up to the riser. I hadn't been the only Jack to notice this man's act of obeisance. Jacks from all over the room had noticed. Soon, they were standing three deep behind me. I'm glad I didn't hold back. Otherwise, instead of having this pig just under my balls I'd be behind somebody else, pissing and moaning about my bad luck. Bad luck doesn't just happen; it is oftentimes made. Well, there he was. A pig in shit.

Eight men were in the tight circle around him. His body began to arch off the riser, rising and falling with the stroke of his fist. Nice tits. I reached down and pulled on one. My buddy across from me reached down and pulled on the other. The blond's body remained in an arched position as he brought his tits up to our hands. A pig! He took his hand off his cock and it twitched with the pulsing of his muscles, bouncing off his stomach, rising and falling back with a life of its own. He was ready to come. But not yet. He knew that he wouldn't get off until he had the cum of every man there, until his pig's body was covered in the slick cum of these men. He was on the Altar. The Priests had him and were going to give him to the gods.

The men had silently surrounded him, but the silence began to be broken by their moans and the heavy breathing. Then the Jacks began to give their praise.

"Hey buddy, you gonna take it all? Huh? Yeah?"

"You want it, don't ya?"

"Fucking pig."

"Hard fucker."

"Awwwgg. . .you bastard, you want my cum, don't ya? Yeah!"

The Jacks were hard at it. The pig wanted it; they were

there to give it to him. But we were all holding. Each and every one of us, even the pig on the riser, was holding. Yeah, it was too good to release just yet. It wouldn't be long, though, till somebody lost it. Lost control and let his cum cascade onto the Acolyte.

The young man looked up into my eyes, then at my cock. I could tell instinctively that he wanted my cum to be the first to splash onto his body. Everyone around the young man was at a fever pitch, including myself, yet all were holding. As I looked around, I could see that they, too, were waiting for my cue, so that they too, could spill their seed onto the temple's sacrifice. It was up to me to start. I could see that I held the power, and because I held them all in my hand, I held them longer. I held, and held. The movement around the table slowed its pace as one and then another brought himself to the point of no return. They were all disciplined and knew they weren't to let loose until I gave the signal.

It wasn't long in coming. I arched my body, lifted myself onto my toes, took a deep breath, and shot a load all over the man. Then it came, spilling over, a flood of cum shooting from all directions directly onto the body and the soul of the gods. Priapus was appeased when the Acolyte, too, shot his load high into the air over himself. His cum fell back, splattering his body, where it mingled and mixed with the life of eternity.

Not a cock shriveled; they jumped and bobbed all around the man. Everyone had his mouth open, filling the room with animal sounds: grunts, growls, and screams. It seemed not to end. The moment that lasts forever came to an end, and slowly we all came back to ourselves and the grimaces all around turned to smiles. Many hands reached down to give the man a love pat or a slap, as the case might be. I reached in and pulled his tits onto my fingers and looked into his eyes. He was grateful, much like a puppy dog. I turned and grabbed a paper towel and wiped sweat, grease, and spent cum from myself.

My mouth was dry again, so I made another trip to the bar. Then I noticed that they were all there. The circle had included all the Jacks on this floor. They had all witnessed and had partaken in the ceremony. In all the times before and since, I have not seen a room full of Jacks so completely of one accord. Usually, two or three, or fives and even tens connect, but the whole room had never been together like that before. It warmed me to the soul to have been a part of such a large jackoff scene. I have made love to 1500 men at once when I have jerked off on a night club stage in New York, but never had I seen so many come so much. I'd be gratified tonight before closing my eyes. I gave a big smile and ordered a beer.

One of the Jacks came up to me and began to talk. It was Gary. He was on the steering committee of the Jacks and could be seen almost every meeting at the door checking the members and their guests. Gary had been one of the master-minds of this whole idea. I told him about the scene that had just passed and thanked him again for allowing me the privilege to be a member of one of the best men's clubs in America.

He told me that the club was at full membership and had become so popular that he now had to turn people away at the door. When I expressed my disappointment at that, he explained to me that the physical space could not accommo-date all those who wanted to join. It is a problem, I suppose. I suggested that he put their names and phone numbers on a list and try to set up another club, the Manhattan Jacks or the Jersey Jacks. Gary gave me some more information about the growing numbers at the buddy clubs like the San Francisco Jacks. It is a movement whose time has come.

The blond man had finished cleaning himself. In other times, I'm sure any one of us would have lent him a tongue to help. He walked up to me, and I noticed that he was about my height, a good-sized man. He grabbed my hand with his and we shook.

"Thanks," he said. "It was great."

"It sure was," I replied.

"I almost didn't get in. I'm from Seattle and I'd heard about the Jacks. I had a real hard time even finding where you all meet. Well, I finally made it to the door, but the doorman wouldn't let me in because I'm not a member. I talked real fast, but he was really a stickler. When I mentioned that I was from Seattle, that did it. He let me in as his guest. I'm glad I made it."

"Well, you made the rest of us fairly happy too," I replied. "Do you realize the sensation that you created here tonight?"

"Isn't it like this all the time?"

"Well, for the most part, yes. But your little show on the riser will be hard to follow. How do you feel about being the center of all that attention?"

"Well, it's not Seattle. Now that I've seen what the New York Jacks are like, I'd like to get a club going there."

We talked a while longer. While we were talking, he saw another group forming and set out to join them. I took another drink and began to think about the night and the Jacks. I felt as if I had been away, had been to many ports of call, and now I was home. Here were men who were of a like mind and who know what they like and they go for it. A structured club of loners who have come together. ▼

GILGEMESH

Gilgemesh

❖ ❖ ❖ ❖ ❖

My senses are reeling. The discovery of this text in the bottom of Professor Scott's locker, along with his personal notes, has stunned me. A respected member of academia and a world renowned archaeologist, Professor Scott was obviously more than an ivory tower scholar—there was a very human side to him. I had known this since the first day of my first class with him nearly four years ago—when he urged all of us students to feel free to call him "Dad," in the field.

During Christmas break, I had heard reports that "Dad" was ill, and when I returned to the campus, I was surprised to find a message waiting for me to call him. Of course, I did so at once, and during the ensuing conversation, his voice was laced with a certain urgency. It seemed that he needed some papers from an antique Macedonian chest he kept in his faculty office. Would I go there and bring them to him? From the tone of his request, I concluded at once that they were very private. Of course, I agreed to oblige him, flattered that he had entrusted me with the task.

As I entered the silent office, I thought about the last four years in which "Dad" had enriched my life. Always bold with a secret smile, "Dad" had long been my idol. And I was not alone in my admiration for the man. The young men in his classes had always swarmed around him, hanging on his every word, treasuring every moment with him—for all too often, he would suddenly vanish to a site halfway around the world.

I found the chest, opened it, lifted out the sheaf of papers he had described to me. The opening page had only one word written on it—"Foreword"—in the professor's distinctive handwriting. I turned the page and began to read:

In the Fourth Millennium before Christ, there lived in Ancient Sumer a king called Gilgemesh. We know this because archaeologists have found clay tablets, a chronicle of events purported to be the oldest writings of humankind, that tell the story of this king. My following adaption of the *Epic of Gilgemesh* transcends the language of the translators and the thousands of years that the clay tablets were buried.

The tablets were transcribed in the Second or Third Millennium B.C., after having been handed down through word of mouth. Not all of the tablets have been found, so the full story of Gilgemesh is still not known. Those tablets that we do possess have been corroborated by the findings of other sets of tablets in several different sites and in several different languages. The general impression that we have of Gilgemesh, the King, and Enkidu, the King's companion, is that they were heterosexual. In every translation, the translator, using modern mores and literary skills, has mistranslated the *Epic*.

Before Christ, the fabric of society was much different from today. It is hardly surprising that words 6,000 years old could be mistranslated. To tell the real story, I have read between the lines and adapted the current translations to tell the real story of the *Epic*.

The names of gods, people, and places—and the grammar—is strange for those of us who occupy the time, space and language of the twentieth century. The time, space, and language of *Gilgemesh* were very early in the history of humankind, when priests first used language to keep secret the mysteries only they enjoyed. Only those who could decipher the strange markings knew—those who could read were "in the know." A strange tale, in a strange language, of long, long ago.

What follows was pre-ordained. There was nothing the individuals could do to change their fate. The gods took an active part in the lives of men and their destinies.

I turned a page and began to read Professor Scott's revisionist translation of the Epic:

The gods in Dilmun (the paradise of ancient Sumer) created the most perfect body to give to Gilgemesh. Shamash, the god of the sun, gave Gilgemesh beauty and sun-yellow hair. Adad gave him courage. Gilgemesh surpassed all other men, yet he was still not a god. He roamed the earth and came to rest in the Kingship on the banks of the river Tigris. The city known to Ali Baba as Baghdad was known as Urak to Gilgemesh. No man could withstand the power and the strength of Gilgemesh. Whether by the sword or his arrogance, or his prowess, Gilgemesh took all men. No man was safe, nor were his sons.

Anu, the father of the gods and the patron of Urak, heard the complaints of the men of Urak and took pity. He requested the goddess of creation, Aruru, that she create a man to equal the mighty Gilgemesh. Aruru was also angered with Gilgemesh, for she had once approached him for an encounter and Gilgemesh had repulsed her.

"I have heard of the way in which you treat your men," he

had told her. "No. I will not lie with you."

As with all women who are scorned, Aruru vowed revenge. She flew into the past to the hour of the birth of Gilgemesh and began to mold, out of clay, Enkidu. Enkidu was the twin of Gilgemesh in all ways save one: his hair was dark. Because he was dark, Aruru gave him to the animals. This is how he came to be.

Gilgemesh was lonely. He had had all men. His stormy heart had no equal. He still felt he was less than half of what he could be. Enkidu, too, longed for a comrade, for someone who could understand his heart. The beasts of the field would no longer run with him, for he smelled of the harlot, the harlot that Aruru had tricked him with.

Almost at once, the revengeful goddess had begun to set the world into motion to bring the two together. Her scheme had taken years, but she was patient and revenge would be sweet. She went to Enkidu and told him not to lose heart, for in Urak lived Gilgemesh who was strong and, like the wild bull, he lorded it over all men.

Enkidu called to the harlot to take him to Urak and the man-god, Gilgemesh, then sent the harlot into Urak with a message for Gilgemesh.

The message read: "I am Enkidu. It is not in me to be less than equal to any man. Gilgemesh, I challenge you to battle in hand to hand combat. I have heard of your disdain for your fellow men, and I am here at the crossroads awaiting your arrogance."

Gilgemesh was only too glad to hear of the challenge. Now his heart was happy.

Anu, the god of Urak, was also pleased. The two men, reflections of each other, could contend together, leaving the men of Anu's Urak in quiet.

The men of Urak, and their sons too, gave a collective sigh of relief.

When Enkidu saw the great Gilgemesh approach, he

called out, "Gilgemesh, you arrogant ass. You have met your match. It is I, Enkidu. I challenge you to make me eat the dust in the roads of your land. It won't be easy. When I'm finished with you, your ass will be dripping my cum into the dust of your roads."

Gilgemesh replied, "Ha. . .Enkidu, you think because you have lain with the lion you can lay me. Come on, you bastard of the gods. It will be your ass dripping with my cum."

Perhaps never again would the world see such a battle. All the battles that ever were or were to be would pall in comparison.

As they began to circle, Gilgemesh and Enkidu released their cloaks and threw them to the winds. Each could see the prowess of the other's manhood. Their cocks grew hard and turned into ax handles. The gods had done well with their creations.

The two daemons of the gods circled one another, each looking for the other's guard to let down, and at the same time, appraising the work the gods had done. Each looked for the opening that would allow him to slip in and mount the other, to push into the dust the face of the other, and then to take his ass.

The two finally came together in an explosion of arms and legs. The battle waged from the early morning to just before sunset. Each attempt to top the other was feigned as each would tackle one another, the defense more fierce than the aggression. The two were so evenly matched that neither could gain the top. Their muscles strained, their breaths shortened, they gasped for air. Still, they came together and fought as neither had fought before. The blood engorged their muscles, their cocks responded, and each thrust from their bodies hardened the resolve of each to gain the top. They came together again and again. Their cocks hardened into one another's body. The veined muscles of arms, legs, and cocks intermingled until the blend was so perfect that they seemed to be one. And so it went, hour after hour.

The sun was near to setting when the two settled into one another. Not an ounce of strength was to be had from both the men. It was over; the two were matchless. They lay exhausted, catching their breath and lying in each other's arms.

"You're a son of the gods," Gilgemesh said as he put his tongue into Enkidu's mouth. "I'm going to mount your ass and then you're going to mount me."

With that statement still on his lips, Gilgemesh grabbed Enkidu and turned his stomach to the dust. Enkidu gave himself to the great Gilgemesh. He pushed his ass into Gilgemesh's cock and felt the cockhead enter him as he relaxed for the first time that day. He took that ax-handle cock up inside himself. This, this, the gods had made him for this. They had created him special to take this man's cock, this god's cock up his ass. Enkidu opened his mouth, and the screams from within were heard in Dilmun.

Anu, the father of the gods knew that never again would the men of Urak, fathers and sons, ever quiver in fear of the might of Gilgemesh. Gilgemesh had finally met his match. The bond was sealed, and together, Enkidu and Gilgemesh would be legend in the annals of humankind.

Enkidu ate the dust of the road and spurted the cum of Gilgemesh's passion into the dust and muddied his belly with the spurting seed of the gods. The beasts were forgotten as he lay under the body of the man, the beast, the god that was Gilgemesh.

Gilgemesh who had never submitted to god or beast or man wanted to experience the same pleasure he had just given to his comrade, Enkidu. But first, the powerful Gilgemesh lifted Enkidu to the sky in his mighty arms and thanked the gods for their deliverance of him from the petty stagnation of men. At last Gilgemesh felt released.

"Fuck me, Enkidu. Fuck me as I fucked you. Stick your ax-handle cock into my ass. Let me submit myself to you in obeisance to the gods for our creation. Give me the pleasure that only the gods allow. Fuck me, you son of the gods."

Enkidu dropped from the arms of his lover and bent the man-god over so that his hands rested in the dust of the road and his ass in the air. He spit onto his godhood and shoved it deep into his own private god. Gilgemesh was his. He had his own man, a god. He thrust into Gilgemesh, pulling out and thrusting in. In and out, he built up his passion, mounting further up into the mangod, the daemon of the gods. Even into the heat of the match, Enkidu had not put his strength as he was now putting into the fucking of Gilgemesh. The gods in Dilmun, on the earth and in the underworld, gave Enkidu the strength to fuck the arrogance from the ass of his comrade.

Gilgemesh had never experienced the pleasure of giving to someone. His ass was his alone until that moment. Gilgemesh remembered, though, that he was conquered not by the strength of man or gods, but by pleasure. He gave himself to his brother, his comrade, his lover. Soon, Gilgemesh felt the groans and screams of pleasure welling up from within his guts. He opened his mouth, and the heavens trembled from the sounds emanating from the guts and soul of Gilgemesh. His seed spurted to the ground as his pleasure mingled with the groans and screams of Enkidu. Wave after wave rousted the two twins, and the universe resounded with their cries of pleasure.

Gilgemesh collapsed into the dust of the road. The cum from Gilgemesh and Enkidu turned the road into a swamp, and the two rolled in their muddy cum, which completely covered the lovers as they locked into one another's arms and embraced. Too long had they been separate selves, too long had the gods separated them. Never could they be separated. None, not man or god, could force them from one another. The two were one.

This is crazy. I would never have taken the translation in this way. But now, after "Dad" has led the way, of course, I see how the words have come together. The etiology is there for us to find the true heart of the story. In all of the earlier translations, the influence of heterosexuality gave the nuances of the language different meanings. Gilgemesh and Enkidu were not merely friends.

Wait a minute. What really is a friend? I stood up, moved behind "Dad's" desk, and found a dictionary. Even in modern day English, the definition begins: "friend (frend), n.[ME. frend; AS. freond, friend, lover; akin to G. Freund; formed, ppr. of the GME, v. "to love." I close the weighty book and replace it on the shelf, contemplating what I have just learned. How far does one go after love—all the way? Even to physical love?

In all cultures past and present, there have been areas that have never been fully or accurately explored. As an archaeology student, I know that even today in cultures that exist in the jungles of Borneo and in South America, scientists will not pursue exploration in many areas because of the forbidden nature of such aspects as cannibalism or man love.

We have always had a heterosexual view of mankind. Why, until just a few years ago, even *The New York Times* would not print the word *gay*. Any view not heterosexual did not get printed. Future archaeologists would have trouble seeing our society as it really is by reading *The New York Times*. And if we can't see our own society, then how can we possibly see any society, past, present, or future?

After a moment, I pick up the sheaf of papers once more. This translation by "Dad" kindles a fire in me. I cannot help but wonder: What if all the translations of all the literatures of all the world were influenced in this way? What great stories have been changed to protect the "innocence" of the reader? My mind cannot conceive of the gross neglect of literature through a widespread determination to put an alternate point of view out of sight, out of mind, out of hetero-sexual society.

I pull out the second chapter of "Dad's" *Gilgemesh* epic. It concerns the Minotaur, and I think back to my studies of early Crete. Early tales of the Minotaur abound: the legends surrounding Theseus and the bull from the sea, the bull leapers in the wall mosaics in the Minos Palace on Crete, where the legends of the Minotaur supposedly began. Man's fascination with the creature that was half-man, half-bull pervades all history.

And here in my hands, I realize, "Dad" is finding the source of all those legends in the deserts of ancient Sumer. Here is the real history of mankind. For wasn't it on the Island of Thebes where men would congregate without the presence of women?

I begin to read again:

Gilgemesh was angry. The labyrinth of the Minotaur was fouled with the stench of bodies rotting for centuries. He and Enkidu were late. Already the youths, the young men of the King's retinue, were scattered through the labyrinth trying to hide from the scourge of the Minotaur. Gilgemesh grabbed Enkidu's arm only slightly to get him to move into the left channel. He had heard danger. They crept to where they could look around the corner to spy the lighted cavern. Gilgemesh took the top, and Enkidu the bottom. The cock of Gilgemesh came to rest on Enkidu's shoulder. Before looking, Enkidu stretched his lips to the head of the cock and kissed it. The two demi-gods were never far apart. They seemed to move as one body, one mind.

As Enkidu looked, he heard the terrible braying of an animal, as if two separate voices made the noise. The scream-yell began to become more resonant with a beat like a drum and more recognizable as a maddened bull rutting.

There before them was chained a young man of maybe twenty. Still no hair on his chest. He was bent over a rock with his arms and legs chained. His ass in the air was filled with the cock of one of the biggest white bulls either had ever seen. Only the head of the bullcock was in the man, who had fainted. Then, suddenly, the bull began to change shape. A man whose skin had never seen the light of day began to merge with the bull. The mighty rear legs of the bull became very hairy with white, egg-white hair. The legs were the most magnificent that either Gilgemesh or Enkidu had seen on any man. As the forms merged in and out of the other, the voice became more hoarse, more rapid. The ass was split, and the bullcock that had yet to change to mancock began to penetrate. Then the man-bull shoved it all in and even though the youth was dead, noise came from his throat as air rushed from the dead lungs and the weight of the man-bull crushed what little life was left out of the boy.

The audible gasp of the two intruders brought the bull to its four feet, as he reared off the back of the boy. The bullcock continued shooting and shooting.

As long as the man-bull had been fucking, the images merged. But never did the head with the huge horns (or the bullcock) change. Promptly the intruders saw the bull dominate as he turned to them, the bull roar of orgasm changing to the roar of challenge.

The cocks of Gilgemesh and Enkidu touched as they both stood to face the bull. Both men were panting, their cocks hardened by what they were seeing, and displayed for the bull to see. Being of the same size in all ways, the twin gods knew they were in for it, because this bull was not a fattened, wizened, old bull but one in its prime, standing almost as tall as a horse. The hefty flank muscles and front shoulders made the bull seem as wide as the palace gate. The hard bullcock didn't shrink a bit, either. It got harder and redder. The veins on the cock showed purple through the white, white flesh and were as big as small tree limbs. Weighted down, the cock neared the ground as it came down from the milk-pail sized balls, hard and throbbing. A man's voice came from the roaring bull.

"Two of you will not save you from me. I'll ravage one while the other looks on. Then I'll save him from the last thrust of my bullcock, so that he can watch the other split as my cock impales him, and then my horns will gut him as I come and come over, in, and around you both."

Gilgemesh ran and leaped. He grabbed the outspread horns with his huge arms and threw his body over the top of the bull, his own head close to the bull's. As he flipped over, Gilgemesh's legs were spread wide as he sprawled lengthwise over the top of the head of the bull. As he landed, his spread out legs grabbed the haunches of the bull, and his huge arms still held the bull by the horns. Now, Gilgemesh was learning the tricks of bull riding.

Enkidu had sprinted to the rear of the bull, grabbed the flinging tail, quickly wrapped the tail around the balls and pulled tight, and held on. In a quick moment, he let go of the tail with one hand and reached quickly to the cock flailing in his face. He grabbed the end of the bullcock in his big, meaty hand and used all his strength to squeeze. As he pulled with all the strength of his arm, the weight of his body, and the force of gravity, the bull whirled his weight to get rid of his tormentors. The six-hundred pounds of the twins flew into the air, as the bull seemed to explode from everywhere. Their ears rang as the bull roar came back at them from the walls. Soon echo waves came back from the depths of the caverns in the labyrinth, and then the screams of the frightened youths who could hear the dead boys' screams still, youths lost in the labyrinth, yet to be caught by the Minotaur and locked in with no escape.

The twins bounded from wall to floor and then up into the positions for round two. This time it was Enkidu who bounded off the horns onto the monster's back, facing the tail, which he again wrapped around the balls, and this time, the cock as well. Gilgemesh grabbed for the rope thrown over the horns and then lunged to wrap the rope around a boulder. Gilgemesh then ran over and threw another rope to Enkidu.

Enkidu, holding the ball-cock rope with one hand, used the other to keep hold of the tail. The bullcock and the balls were now as red as the sun at setting when the forests burn. They had swelled enormously. Enkidu had to let go of the tail to loosen the loop of the rope. Quickly, he took the enlarged rope loop and encircled not only the balls but the cock as well. Enkidu tumbled off the back of the bull, and with another quick loop, the bull was secured fore and aft.

By then, the ball-cock rope had tightened to where the cock and balls could easily be lopped off. If the bull stumbled, he could lose his balls and cock. The bull came to a rest in a very awkward position, and his wailing bull's voice quickly began speaking the human language of the twins. "Quick, give me slack, or whilst I become a man again, I'll surely be killed," he begged.

The form was beginning to change again. The bull-man was coming back. Gilgemesh quickly took another rope and hog-tied the bull front feet to back feet, as Enkidu took the cock-ball rope from around the rock and wound it around his own body. The body of the bull became more and more man-like. The legs and hooves of the bull became hands and legs, although his cock and balls didn't change, and neither did his head.

The bull man became more and more man. Tied hand and foot and head and cock, the bull-man was in a natural arch. He couldn't move a muscle. Enkidu took the ball-cock rope and wrapped his own cock and balls in a slip knot. If the bull moved a millionth of a hectare, Enkidu would know. With the man-bull's positioning, his ass was now in the air. Neither Gilgemesh or Enkidu had ever seen a man as muscled as this one was. He was as large as the bull, his chest enormous, with a row of tits on each side of his chest. Enkidu's cock throbbed harder and harder as he watched the metamorphosis. Gilgemesh reached into his traveling bag, brought out a pot of grease, and began to work it over his hands and arms. He walked up to the bull-man and slapped the broad nose hard with his fist.

"Now, you bastard beast, it's your time. Enkidu, tie all the tits together to his cock and balls." As Enkidu obeyed him, Gilgemesh went to the rear of the animal, reached down, and picked up the rest of the coil of rope which bound the hands and feet of the beast. He reached into the pot and slapped grease on the asshole. Gilgemesh could see the beast's heartbeat in the puckered hole. He began to beat the ass. The pulsing asshole opened wider. Gilgemesh clasped his hands together, straightened his arms, and ran his body into the hole.

The man-bull didn't even move from the onrush of Gilgemesh's body into him nor flinch as both of the man's arms plunged forward into his depths. As Gilgemesh came to rest, the bull swayed back, and Gilgemesh felt the hole around his arms begin to envelop him to his shoulders. The bull-cock swelled even more and almost at once began to explode. Enkidu rolled under the bull-man and backed onto the bull-cock. The heavy, thickened head entered Enkidu, not easily but well. He backed harder onto the bull-cock. The overflow oozed from his hole and ran down Enkidu's leg.

Soon, Gilgemesh jabbed his cock and his balls into the bull's ass. The trio's ecstasy flowed from their mouths, their cockheads, their bodies, and their souls.

The gods were jealous. But they were satisfied. The Minotaur had been tamed.

As I reach down into the chest to replace the papers, I use my other hand to plunge into my sweat pants and find my hard cock waiting. Both Gilgemesh tales have unleashed unknown passions within me. Just touching my throbbing cock is enough to bring torrents of cum near the brink of exploding. I let go of myself and think again about the tales. The Minotaur has really been a one-of-a-kind experience. Reading the translation has been like a movie. I can still see every detail in my mind's eye, especially the Minotaur bound forever to these twin gods, chained and helpless, his hole nothing more than an entrance for them. I stuff my cock back into my shorts and try to make my sweats presentable for travel in public.

I hurry to my car, open the trunk, bring out a length of rope, and place it in my briefcase. Back at the professor's office, I find a note I have not see before, a note from "Dad" asking how I have responded to his new translation.

I look about and begin to move the furniture around. In a few minutes, I am ready. I turn on the desk lamp and turn off the overhead fluorescents. I lay the desk lamp on its side and cover it with my red hankie. I move toward the wall, and a few moments later, I hear the sound of "Dad's" whistle floating down the hallway.

The Gilgemesh epic was true. There had actually been a kingdom ruled by two kings, long before Alexander, long before the pyramids. My reverie on this subject, however, is interrupted by the professor opening the outer door to the office. He seems surprised to see the red glow, but he remains casual as he observes me, his prize undergraduate, roped to the wall. He closes the door, locks it, and pulls the specially created draperies, as he has done so many times before. I like "Dad" for many reasons, not the least of which is that he has always indulged so many of my fantasies. ▼

❖ ❖ ❖ ❖ ❖ ❖
NEUTRINO
❖ ❖ ❖ ❖ ❖

Neutrino

❖ ❖ ❖ ❖ ❖

Jon moved slowly. The heavy gravity of Ganymede pulled him closer to his objective; months of weightlessness held him back. His muscles were slow to respond. The inactivity of suspended animation was felt even in his mind. Still, he knew it would be only moments before he would awaken fully. The first sensation of life was his throbbing cock. Months of inactivity in his sex organs had always brought on the need of sexual release immediately upon awakening.

That need posed enormous problems in the beginning of the colonization of space. Men and women in sexual frenzies had begun population explosions that threatened the survival of colony after colony. Jon had remembered the telenews of the first colony's food riots. Of course, the loss of the supply ship was the more meaningful disaster, but coupled with all the new children, the riot of the colony had been a definite setback. Then too, the psych people were sure that instinctual heterosexual territory requirements had begun the panic. That had been good news for Jon. The first colony had been abandoned. The setback in the program was compensated for by recruiting the first all-Theban space corps, and the first military use of the Thebans would be in space. The shake-up after the riots had changed all the schedules, and Jon had moved from the bottom of the list to the top. Because Jon had not fit the heterosexual mode, all the academia in the world didn't matter.

Now it did matter. The colonies had to be settled by the Theban corps until such time as the colonies could not only sustain themselves, but become way stations of supply for the outer colonies like the one on Ganymede. Jon had been in charge of the second Mars colony and had proved the Theban stratagem as a viable alternative.

The other problems for colonization were actually minor except for one. The suspended animation seemed to work all right on earth, but when actually applied in space, the lack of gravity did something to the chemicals in the drugs used to make the suspended animation systems work. The psych people had worked with Tibetan monks, and the problems that had been attenuated in Space Suspended Animation Systems (SSAS) were now gone. It was a simple solution: a combination of meditation and self-hypnosis till the heartbeat was brought to within one or two an hour. Without gravity, blood didn't drift to the bottom of the body. The only side effect was the almost conscious activity in and out of dream states for the entire voyage.

Another side effect was the horniness at voyage's end. Men tended to wet dream their way to the stars, hence the sexual activity at voyage's end. Compounding this problem was the methamphetamine compounds used to bring them out of the self-induced suspended animation (SISA).

Jon's throbbing cock brought him back from the reverie. The new colony was his second beginning. His crew had been picked not only for their knowledge of space colonization, but for their psychological profile as well. There had been Theban corps dropouts, mainly due to the discovery of heterosexual vestiges in some of them. What was left was a group of men not only dedicated to the colony but also dedicated to each other as Thebans—men who loved men enough to die for each other, but not to kill each other.

The canopy began to slip away from Jon's body. The rush of oxygen into the opening chamber did much to vitalize Jon's muscles. The injection of moments before was crystallizing his whole body. SSAS began to rapidly fade, and his thoughts become lusty and passionate. The vibrancy was glowing from toe to head. Jon's body jerked. The head of his cock became even more turgid, like a balloon ready to pop. He had never been under for such a long time—no one had. Coming out of it had never been this strong, Jon noted as he opened his eyes. The chemical coursing through his veins was stronger than he had ever experienced. His body jerked again and again. Jon bolted upright. His lungs filled with rarefied air. His cock was aching for release.

As Jon became more cognizant of life, he looked around at the other sleepers. Mac was next to him, so close as to be almost touching. Jon looked through the canopy at Mac. The crystallized atmosphere clung to the canopy's clear plastic but was rapidly vaporizing. Jon could see his buddy's body clarifying through the dense vapor and crystal. Jon never tired of watching the metamorphosis. The first response to coming awake always showed in the cock. As the blood would begin to flow again, the cock would become turgid and begin to throb with every heartbeat. When the blood began to move and course through the veins, building the pressure, the syringe would release the chemical into the blood stream.

Jon watched the syringe withdraw from Mac's arm. The chemical was released. Mac's cock responded by jerking into the air above his body. The air in the chamber was clear now and Mac's canopy began to withdraw. Jon moved his eyes from the exploding cock and looked into the face of Mac in time to see his eyelids flutter once and then jerk wide open.

Jon reached out with his hand and grabbed Mac's cock, then leaned into Mac and kissed his lips. Jon's ass began to twitch, but he had to restrain himself. There were five other men to be tended to. Mac began to jerk, and Jon left him to begin the process with the others.

"We have to work quickly," thought Jon. "Otherwise the rushes won't correspond."

Jon knew that the complications could be enormous if they were all at different levels of awareness and life. The beginning rushes were still building in Jon. He had never experienced a cock as hard as this one—but then he had never before been under for five years. Mars had been only two years. The urgency of his cock made him hurry. He looked over to Mac in time to see Mac jerk upright. Everything was going well. Mac climbed from his cocoon and began to help Jon with the rest of the crew. Jon scanned the instruments hooked to his crew. Good, all was in order. Soon the other five canopies began to clear while the crystals vaporized.

Jon took one last look at the instruments before he reached out and grabbed Mac. They kissed once more before moving into the Ultra-Chamber, their cocks leading the way. They halted under the lamp and stood still with their arms and legs outstretched beside one another while they were flashed. The layer of dead skin burned away in the flash, and their bodies became red in the diminishing light. Jon opened his eyes and looked at Mac, then led him into the vacuum chamber where the remaining powdered skin was whisked from them and a light coating of unguents sprayed upon their bodies. Jon looked through the chambers to where the rest of the crew was awakening.

Jon's cock throbbed at a faster pace. The chemicals were at the optimum now and would not decrease for hours. His crew was already assembling beneath the Ultra-Flash. Each one seemed to be all cock. Their bodies seemed to be transforming in waves to throbbing cocks, but it was the chemical and his imagination. The crew members were beautiful to behold. Jon closed his eyes as the red light blinked the warning of the impending flash.

Everyone knew that the need to speak was not necessary. At this time, the concentration of thought to speech would take away from the actions at hand. Jon slipped into the arms of Mac. They kissed again, hungrily devouring each other. Cock against cock, Jon pulled Mac into the mat room. All was as they had left it in what seemed only moments ago, but was actually five years past. Everything was ready for them.

The importance of this mission demanded that the crew be at least compatible sexually as well as able to handle their particular specialties to allow the shipmates to obtain the goals of the mission. Mac and Jon were shipmates from the beginning and had bunked together in the first year at UASA, United Aeronautical and Space Aviation school. They had come to share their lives and their careers. They were well matched, as Jon, the pilot, always needed Mac, the navigator. The rest of the crew was a mixed lot because of their different career specialties. What was most extraordinary was that in one way or another they had all shipped together before. There was no mystery here.

Jon and Mac interrupted their almost panicky sex to rest a moment and watch the crew come into the mat room. It was almost a moving orgy. Crazy Dan had his cock in Jack's ass as they walked forward together. Dan was guiding Jack, who was simultaneously bent over to Stan with his mouth on the largest cock of the group. The other two were in a world of their own. These two had been partners longer than Jon and Mac had. They were brothers, and for the most part, if it had to do with the mission, they were right on top of it. Otherwise they were always together and in their own little world. They even had their own private language.

Mac turned over and raised his middle off the floor while Jon crawled under and took Mac's cock into his mouth. Dan pulled out of Jack and knelt into Mac's ass. Stan pillowed Mac's head and mouth onto his cock as he lay in front of Mac, while Jack pulled Jon's cock into his mouth and Stan took Jack's cock into his. It wasn't a practiced and routine thing that they were doing. Still, it worked, and with minor variations and adjustments, they would remain in these basic positions for sometime. The ebb and flow of the sexuality, the wake up drugs, the personal preferences, the almost imperceptible communications of the group melded the quintet into what seemed to be an organism that was one instead of five separate ones. Seen from above, it would seem to be just that: one organism. The cum flowed from one to another in a circle. A body in the organism would begin to thrust, and the next body would thrust into the next. A groan would follow a groan. A flexed muscle would follow a flexed muscle. For hours, they would be this way. The flow and ebb of oceans repeated here on the mats, as life into life flows and ebbs.

At last the buzzer sounded. Mac and Jon left the group on the mat for the control panels of the cockpit. It was time to turn off the automatic pilot and begin the mission. The serious nature wiped all but the grins on their faces from the minds of the two on whom the safety of their shipmates and the success of the mission rested. The other five could languish a few hours more before their part of the mission would take them out of the mat room to their respective work areas. This was a Theban crew. Proud of their opportunity, proud of their work, proud of themselves. Alexander The Great's army of lovers conquering the Universe. Their mission might fail, but they would do the job to the best of their ability and not bring shame to their shipmate lovers. They are the Patroclus and Achilles, Alexander and Hephaistion of their time. They are Thebans, the most highly decorated unit of the UASA. ▼

THE
ESSAYS

LEGACY

Legacy

❖ ❖ ❖ ❖ ❖

We were so poor that on Christmas day when I woke up, I only had my cock to play with.

In that one sentence you will find the complete story of my life. I suppose that is the way it is with most boy children. Our first real passion in life, besides chocolate, is our cock. And then one morning (and every morning thereafter) it wakes up hard. . .

Growing up in my family, with a patriarchal grandfather who is a fundamentalist preacher, did something to my psyche. So did growing up in the fifties. I was twenty-four before I had satisfactory, guiltless, gay sex. I'm now over fifty, and only half of that life has been sexual. Being HIV positive for ten years, another fifth of that life has been under the specter of AIDS. Yet through it all, since puberty, my hard cock has been raging.

I think of the tangible legacies of those who have built nuclear power plants for GE, those who have flown to the moon and beyond, and then I think of me and my raging hard cock. What legacy will I leave posterity?

And then I think of a party in New York City at the Underground night club. It was in an old bank building on Union Square that had been hollowed out. The basement was a dance floor, the ground floor only a stage hanging out over the dance floor. The second floor was the VIP lounge that, too, overlooked the basement dance floor. All the broken brick walls were outlined in pastel neons and have been preserved for posterity in a quick blip in a film called *Liquid Sky*. As with many things, the Underground is part of the good old days and is no more.

The party was called "Steam." Gay men were handed towels at the door. There were lockers for their clothes, and off the basement dance floor was a hot tub.

At 2:00 A.M., The Manhattan Transfer had the dance floor in the palms of their hands as they slid out on the overhanging stage to please the hot crowd of sweaty, steamy men dancing in their "Steam" towels. At 4:00 A.M., Richard Locke slid out onto the stage above the trampling, hot, sweaty, steaming men with nothing but his hard cock pointing toward the heavens, and to the hot, throbbing music from the sound track of his latest film, *Heatstroke*, the towels began dropping. Soon, the men began to stroke to the music along with the man with the hard cock above them. The flesh, the fantasy, and the reality began blending to a ride through the cosmotic heavens—all blending together in one love party.

A tangible legacy? I think so. I feel there was a leap forward in social and cultural levels in those "heydays." My films and stage shows were a part of the warp and woof that made up the quilt of our times.

As I stroked with the five hundred men below me to the beat of the music and each other, I didn't think of these things. It is only now in retrospect that I can see the enormity of what was happening. These men and I were celebrating a freedom seldom given to men. It was extraordinarily mind-boggling, what we were doing.

The technology of film and video has brought this same kind of mind-boggling freedom right into everyday life and even into our homes. When I first made a film, I thought it would be only a part of the sleaze in big city arcades, a loop providing endless fantasies. But the producers budgeted for public relations and spent $12,000 on subway ads on Christopher street. *Variety*, the voice of New York's entertainment world, reported Dino de Laurentis' *King Kong* as the #1 Box Office and *Kansas City Trucking Co.* as number fifty at the box office. My film and I had entered the mainstream America.

I began to receive fan letters, many fan letters, actually, and the one I remember most came from a man in Ypsilanti, Michigan. He had driven five hours to see one of my films, and for the few hours he spent with me in the film, he could be himself. Then he went home to his wife and kids. All those years I had spent in denying myself, of denying my very being, came back to me. In liberating myself, I was also liberating others, maybe for only a little time, but as they say, it is better to have loved for a moment than never to have known love at all.

Well some beg to differ. "Sex ain't love," they say. I know better. When I began to love myself, I began to love others. I did it with my whole heart and soul. I have never been sexual with anyone I didn't love, even if only for a moment, or in a crowd, or on the screen, or on a stage. Multiple orgasms can be experienced by multiple people. The more the merrier.

One of my best friends said to me the other day that I had "built my life on sex." My lover picked up on it, and every once in awhile, he uses it as tongue-in-cheek humor. It is not a nuclear power plant or a trip to the moon, but I have no regrets and I'm proud of my contributions.

I have not died of AIDS because my work is, evidently, unfinished. I'm still here, ain't I? I know that when I die, the work will not yet be finished. The work of liberation is never done, and the work with AIDS goes on. Maybe we will go to where there is peace. There is a drive for peace that is within us all, a drive that pulls us along, as a leaf in the wind is pulled into the eddy of forces unknown to us. We are all reaching out to see the unseeable. In any case, we are not allowed the rest and peace we seek while here in this life. We are a restless breed. A hard cock is nature's way, and that is the power of our restlessness. My advice: Have friends, be proud and have no regrets.

A frog has the ability to see only six feet in front of his nose. He never has, and possibly never will, see the stars that are very plain for us to see, and with future technologies, even for us to reach out to. I wonder what there is in this life that we can't see. Humanity has a better side that we don't see enough of. We call it altruism.

I didn't do it for the money. There was very little money made during the days of my career, all things considered. I don't quite think it's all altruism either. I became a star because I said "Yes" when I was asked to be in a film. People liked me. I was asked to make another, and again I said "Yes." The time for a person like me had arrived. Had I said "No," then another person would be writing this biography. I probably would have said no to the second film, had I not received the letters, especially the Ypsilanti letter. I felt needed and I felt that somewhere out there is a frightened kid who might wander into a theatre and see me, and his life could change. Just yesterday, another person told me that I brought him out when he was a teenager. Others have said, "Keep doin' it, Richard. You're makin' us older fellas look good." Exhibitionism is great. Applause can make an orgasm very exciting. In the end, all things considered, I didn't do it for the money. ▼

THE
CENTURY
THEATRE

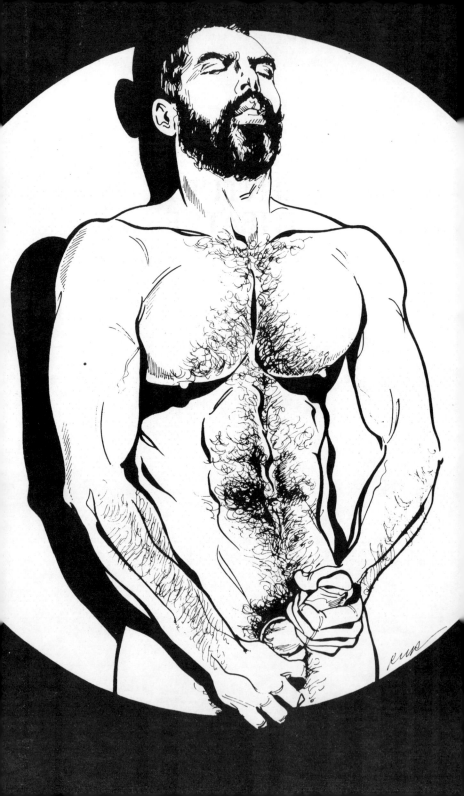

The Century Theatre

❖   ❖   ❖   ❖   ❖

A few years back, Nick Rodgers was the art director of the strip revues at the Century Theatre in Los Angeles. While he was the director, the show at the Century was a hard place to match for professional go-go dancing. The quality of the acts was consistently of the caliber of "Chippendale's," the straight club for women only.

Nick, like myself, had run the gamut of the theatres. In New York alone, we had both played the Adonis, the Show Palace, the Ramrod, the Follies, and all the other Times Square theatres.

In those days, besides New York City, there were the cities on the road. There was The Follies in Washington, D.C. and its counterpart in Pittsburgh. It was always changing its name. It was in Pittsburgh where I met, for the first time, a few of the women on the burlesque circuit: Chesty Morgan and the woman who appeared on a television program, "stripping for Christ." She was "for real." They certainly were not Lily Saint Cyr or Gypsy Rose Lee, but they had their own style. They played the straight theatre below the gay theatre. Chesty

Morgan had a seventy-two-inch chest—eat your heart out, Arnold.

Then in Chicago, there was the Bijou. Yes, I even played the Bijou. From there, we go to San Francisco where the choices were very limited. The Nob Hill was not a good place to do business, and after all, it is called "Show Business." The old Screening Room, where Hollywood movies were screened by "in-town movie producers" had become Savages, where my show premiered the opening of a new generation of gay porno theatres. Savages was also not good to do business with, at least for me. And, last but not least, there was The Century. Artie Bressan and I appeared there in person to talk about filmmaking in general and our latest movie at the time, *Daddy Dearest*. Artie was a good filmmaker—his films are always there with you, even today.

Finally, the circuit was complete with The Century Theatre in Los Angeles. It was the creme de la creme. Both the San Francisco and the Los Angeles Century Theatres were owned by the same man. He was always worrying about cum stains on the velour seats. Both theatres had wide screens, so wide that all the filmmakers took into consideration the size of the screen when framing their movies. If they failed to take this consideration, the action would just sort of float off the screen so that it couldn't be seen at either Century. Big cocks were *big*. Today, both theatres are no longer in business; the L.A. Century is dark and the S.F. Century has become a straight porn house.

In those years, the police department was very crazy about what could and couldn't be seen. Wakefield Poole, the director of *Boys in the Sand*, told me that he had to cut the scene with the brothers fistfucking in *Take One*. He said, "It won't play L.A." Then and there, I decided that one day I'd be in a film that was titled, *It Won't Play L.A.*

But we're getting off the subject. I had to lay a little groundwork, so that you could better get into the following true story.

I have changed some of the names to protect the guilty. I keep mine in the story only because I put my name on everything I do.

Nick Rodgers had called me and told me that the Century had finally become a private club. In California, what people do in private between consenting adults is no business of the police. This signaled the opening, the liberation of L.A.

No one had yet to reach orgasm on the professional stage in L.A. I was asked to be the first. I came into town to see the beginning of the month-long festival of flesh at the Century. I was to appear the following Saturday. Nick had arranged for about eleven strippers and one or two different guest appearances of well known porn stars every week through the month to celebrate.

The show was quite exciting. The regular strippers, of the ones I remember, included a magician who pulled rabbits out of hats after he had stripped to a G-string. He was muscled like a swimmer—nice pecs and a washboard stomach. A black lamé G-string really set off his beauty and his fantastic physique. I had always looked forward to seeing a "real" body builder do a strip number. He didn't disappoint anybody with his show. Then there was the trapeze artist, and the tumblers. It was very much a strip circus with very hot young men totally enjoying themselves. There was another guy, beautiful, great washboard stomach, tit bars that held gold washers onto the tits (very sexy), and a long uncircumcised cock that held a weight of some sort, and the cock itself was held in by an armor-clad jockstrap. This guy was full of surprises, and you can catch an abbreviated, poorly cut and edited version of the act in a very poor film called *Gayracula*.

Even though the show was very hot stripping, it didn't have any sex. Well, I decided I'd fix that when I brought my New York show, *Saturnalia*, the next week. My guest partner for that show was a guy named Dixon Hardy. Nick told me that Dixon's specialty was sucking himself off. Not only was he going to do this on stage, but the huge screen of The Century would be simultaneously running a film clip in which Dixon would be giving himself a blowjob. The self-suck on the stage was to be done in synchronization with the film. Well, that was going to be a tough act to swallow—I mean, follow. I wanted the first cum shot on the L.A. stage to be mine. I asked Nick to have Dixon follow my act.

Now that you've got the setup, I'll get down to the brass tacks of the event.

There we were. The audience to the rafters. And we still had twenty minutes till curtain. Yeah, a real curtain. For the first time, after playing all the sleaze holes across the country, I had a real curtain on stage. This was the big time. And we had banks of lights. Big lights. Wow! This was going to beat the time I tore the ceiling out of the Ramrod and installed, with my own money, a wonderful lighting system. The original lighting system had replaced the candles that were used by Sarah Bernhardt when she played Times Square. I guess I'm off the subject again. Back to The Century.

I was doing what every director tells you not to do. "Don't peek at the customers through the curtain. If you can see them, they can see you." Behind me, the muscle guy was lifting weights. God, he was built like a brick shithouse. He had the same attitude as a guy who had won the body building championship in Columbus, Ohio a few years back. That champ, in the competition, was shorter than the rest, but he had the body and everytime he would take a new position, he would flesh it out all over. Then the last ounce of energy spent for the pose went to freeze his hard cock. That cock could be seen twitchin' as he changed to the next pose. The champ told Arnold that he was gonna take the title that Arnold had held for so long. Attitude? More than enough.

This guy lifting the weights backstage didn't need any more attitude either, but, like the other champ, you could see it was good attitude. The guy liked himself. He liked being where he was and doing what he was doing. He had pride in himself. And that is what being gay and straight is all about. I think straights would be inclined to deal with gayness more easily if they could have more pride in themselves.

Then there was the magician pulling his different props into place and checking them out.

In the alleyway, the flame thrower was tossing swords into the air, juggling them in a most dangerous way.

We were quite a troupe. I felt good about it all. I was reminded about how good I had felt after my very first appearance onstage at the Follies in Washington D.C. I had come off all over the third row on a sound cue. The audience had been silent. No applause. I was worried. But then the manager had said, "Hey, man, you had them in the palm of your hand. They were stunned. This is the first time in this theatre's history that no one has gone to the glory holes, the orgy room, or for popcorn. For half an hour, they were yours."

Even though I felt good, I still wasn't sure about the worth of my show until one night on a talk show I saw Jack Lemmon being interviewed about his latest flick, *The China Syndrome.* He said he was worried about the film until he watched a sneak preview. He said the audience was so very attentive. And then he said something that I have always kept with me: "You know you've got it. You know you're an artist when you have the audience in the palm of your hand."

In my case, the cock in my hand was the audience, and I was playing them for all they were worth.

I pulled away from the curtain to find my guest partner and Nick coming toward me. Nick introduced him to me, and we went into the wings a little deeper to talk. It seems Dixon had used me to help himself come out. I had been his inspiration. We talked of my movies, and then he told me of his apprehensions. This was his first appearance in front of an audience. He was worried about putting on a good show.

Well, what was I to do? Joe Gage had always used me to get the last scene, the orgy, into high gear. I'd pull it out, and soon the others would follow. That's when Joe would have the camera man move into the arena and the orgy was officially begun.

Very nervously, Dixon opened his pants and brought out this average-sized dick. I began pulling on my cock, and as it began to thicken and grow in length, I looked at Dixon. His vision was centered on my cock. And then that very average Dixon Dick began to grow extraordinarily large. I saw it, but I didn't believe it. I had to touch it, I had to know if it was really real. It got bigger and then harder as I stroked it. I looked at Dixon who raised his eyes to mine. The dick in my hand was as large as it was going to get, or so I thought, but when Dixon looked into my eyes, the cock got harder and harder. The Matterhorn was soft in comparison.

I have had some big cocks in my time, so it wasn't difficult to go down, all the way down, on that big one. I gave it to him, my mouth on his cock, yeah. God, it was good. And even though I had thought it was as hard as it would get, it did get harder. I looked up and his eyes had gone to the back of his head. I pulled out and went down some more. His cock twitched and my head lifted. It was a powerful cock. I gave good head. He gave good cock.

As I pulled off and straightened up, I could see the body builder pumping his arms, the strained stomach muscles with the bronze skin pulling over the flexing washboard stomach. Before I was upright, Dixon was on his knees, pulling my cock right into his throat. What I gave good, he gave better. His blondish head bobbed up and down my shaft, pulling me onto my tiptoes.

There I go getting off the subject again. My cue came up and I went out onto the stage. Every once in awhile I'd glance out of the corner of my eye and see Dixon, stage left in the wings, pulling on that big dick of his. My sound cue for coming seemed to be hours away, and I was already ready to come. The valley of orgasm was almost breached at least ten times before my cue finally came and I could shoot. I blasted the third row again and made my exit.

It was Dixon's turn, and the curtain pulled back to reveal him and his dick sitting on a riser. The audience was ready for it. I could see that many of them had seen the billing and had saved their cum shots for Dixon. The lights spilling from the screen and the stage were enough to make the first row almost as brilliantly lighted as Dixon's dick, which had a follow spot turned down to its smallest size to illuminate that big dick. The first row was sizably strong, too, all of them pulling and jerking with Dixon.

My first time on the stage, I had been as nervous as Dixon was feeling at this moment, but I had reminded him that the audience came to see a good show and was pulling for him and was not at all hostile.

"Give 'em a good show. Put all you have into it. Strut your stuff." I'd told him. "And the audience will always give it back to you. They will echo up to you what you give them. They want you to do well. They're not out to get you."

You couldn't have paid to get a better audience. The magician and body builder had whetted their appetite and got them hard. I had them close to coming, but Dixon was to be the *coup de grace*. The biggest screen in gay porndom was filled with his big cock and bigger mouth. You know the guy must be double-jointed. If I had that big a cock, I could go down on it too—anybody could at least get the head in. But this sucker, he'd go all the way down to the base and just sit there and suck on it. I could see the throat muscles move back and forth on it—just like a snake swallowing a mouse. I could see his throat widen for that big head.

Backstage, still naked and oiled up, the body builder and I were jerking off to Dixon's suck and thrust. Some guy in the front row couldn't handle it. I heard this loud moan and peeked out in time to see this guy stick out his legs and shoot up onto the stage which was no mean feat, as it was four feet away and four feet up. Then another audience stud lost it, and then another. They were like dominoes.

Dixon pulled off to see it and then quickly grabbed his cock with both hands and stuck out his legs. His cockhead began to ooze. It wasn't time for him to come. He was out of sync with the film. The body builder couldn't wait either. He was standing next to me by this time, and I reached out and caught his jism in my hand.

I heard another groan. The groan was loud and amplified. It was the sound track of Dixon's film. The screen was filled with cum coming out of Dixon's mouth, and out there on the stage, the floor was catching the cum that had slipped out of Dixon's mouth and dripped down his cock to fall to the stage.

By this time the stage floor beneath my feet was getting messy, what with my cum and the cum of the body builder. A groan from behind me told me that the magician too had shot his wad. We had all been overcome with the fervor of the exhibition. Those poor velour seats had been righteously inaugurated.

Dr. Art Ullene on the "Today" show, March 11, 1987, advocated abstinence as the only safe way of avoiding the AIDS virus. *Shit, Art, how about playing with yourself?*

After the show, Dixon and I went for a beer, and he related how he had been self-sucking since he was a very little kid. His cock had matured early, probably because he had played with it early. His ability to go to the base was probably because kids are much more limber than adults, and since he did it often and had never gotten out of the habit, it was easy for him to self-suck. Not so easy for me these days. I'm not as well endowed, and the difficulty and exertion begins turning me off before I get the tongue to the head. Oh, well, there are other ways to have fun with yourself, so I'm not that disappointed. ▼

SPORT
FUCKING

Sport
Fucking

❖   ❖   ❖   ❖   ❖

The future for us all, and for sexual liberty, can be health, peace, and love. Liberty literally means "freedom from restrictions." Zen and sexual liberty go hand in hand. How "well" we perform the sex act will set us free of disease. How "well" will give us the liberty we have always sought. We children of gay and sexual liberation are going to grow up, be responsible, and face reality, whether we like it or not.

I have an example of how simple the "how" of sex can lead to disease. Thirty million Americans have herpes. If these people had turned on the lights and had scrutinized their sex partner's body, if they had used a prophylactic, if they had washed with a microbicide before and after sex, their exposure to the herpes could have been eliminated. A simple thing like a light switch, a rubber, or bathing could have saved years of misery for them and freedom from contagion for numerous others. The path of disease transmission can be avoided.

I don't like the term "safe sex." The scientists say that the only safe sex is masturbation; anything beyond that is merely "possibly" safe, or just downright unsafe. Instead, I feel we can use the term "sensible sex," which means good common sense. Sensible sex takes those high risk activities out of the risk category and brings them into the low risk category. It must be remembered, however, that low risk is still a risk.

There has been much grief and sorrow caused by the spectre of AIDS. In order to understand what sensible sex is, we must discuss AIDS, and the transmission of the disease, which we know requires a vehicle to carry the deadly virus into a susceptible person. Specific to AIDS, it is certain that semen and blood are both vehicles. Saliva, urine, ear wax, feces, tears, sweat, any or all could also be the vehicle.

Celibacy is one way to interrupt the transmission of disease. Since for many this is not a viable alternative, not having mucous exchanges is another option. For example, mutual masturbation and frottage is "safe," according to the scientists, but anything beyond this is only "possibly safe."

About twelve years ago I had a friend who jumped off the Golden Gate Bridge. He lived. Thus can it be said that jumping off the Golden Gate Bridge is possibly safe? Is this to say "possibly not safe" as well? I think so. There are risks, for any "body," when sexual activity is anything beyond masturbation, even though precautions have been taken. The responsibility for sexual disease transmission is with the individual. It is his responsibility to protect himself. The only person responsible for a dripping cock is the person with the dripping cock. Precautions must be taken.

I believe it is necessary to hand some of the responsibility for the spread of AIDS to our society's antiquated thinking about morality. Sexually transmitted diseases require the health departments of all government agencies to purvey correct information at all educational levels. Most sadly, we are at the mercy of only a few bigots who control policy, and by politicians who have no balls.

I was present at the San Francisco Human Rights Commission meeting in the spring of 1986, to hear a Mrs. Stone plead for sex hygiene education in schools. Her nineteen year-old son had recently died of AIDS. We teach children how to vote, and yet they can't vote till they are eighteen, yet we can't give them sex hygiene information that might save their lives because some feel that such information lends acceptance to premature sex. Mrs. Stone's son, though fully educated on how to vote, never got the chance to.

Sensible sex is more than simply non-mucous sex. It also encompasses more than a way to get one's rocks off without mucous contact. The only limit to sensible sex is the imagination. Imagination, fantasy, patience, timing, planning, and any number of other things can blend to make a satisfying, caring, sexual encounter without the sterility that is symbolized by "safe sex." Many of the sex acts in the following discussion were developed from experience and imagination. My partners taught me a lot, and with the passage of time they have been improved upon.

For instance, I first tried ballfucking about twelve years ago. It was an excruciating experience. Those moving and slippery globes were unmanageable and almost impossible to get into a tight hole. Eight years later, I found a ball stretcher that enabled me to have more control over those slippery globes, and as well, I'm not quite so anal retentive these days. Ballfucking has become one of my more favorite activities—and there is no mucous contact with ballfucking.

Berkeley's radio station, KPFA, went off the air for forty-five minutes when I was asked about a "safe sex" method.

I replied, "Well there is testicular fornication."

"What's that?" the moderator asked.

"Ballfucking," I replied.

Zaaappppp!

They told me it was a power failure. They didn't really censor me. They censored the audience.

There are many more methods of interrupting the transmission of disease and to still have a satisfying sex life. Use imagination and be inventive. Use your disposable income and be creative. Explore the ethereal side of disease interruptus.

There has been quite a lot *not* said about fisting. Cocksuckers and assfuckers have received guidelines and risk reduction techniques since the beginning of the AIDS crisis., but not the fisters. "They" say that "fisting is extremely dangerous." "They" say this not so much from the standpoint of disease transmission, but from the standpoint that fisting is an ugly sex act.

Handballing or fisting is non-mucous sex (unless you happen to be jerking off with cock and hand inside someone's ass, which is extremely dangerous). Semen and trauma, minute or large, is a bad combination.

But handballing, from the standpoint of disease transmission, is as sensible as anal intercourse with condoms. This is predicated upon the idea that there is no bleeding or trauma to receive the micro-organisms. If you have a cut on your hand, don't stick it in somebody's butt, and don't come in somebody's rectum ever.

A thorough body scrub, especially the hands, nails, and arms, as if you were a surgeon ready to do surgery, is required for minimum hygiene. Use a lubricant dispenser, such as an automotive grease gun. And there should be no "double dipping" into the same Crisco can. Use separate cans and label them with the names of the people involved. Limit yourself to low or no drug intake, so that the bottom is aware of his limits. Have a sensitive partner who cares about your health and his own.

If this is accomplished, there is little to no risk of disease transmission.

Handballing can be suicidal and homicidal, or a reflection of the two, depending on the people who engage in the activity. It can also be a healthful, recreational, sport fuck. It really boils down to the two or more people involved in it. It can be mind-boggling for the top as well as the bottom when you reach the limits of the activity. It can be religious. It can be exactly what you want it to be.

Before I started handballing, my asshole seemed always to be either going into or coming out of a hemorrhoidal stage. My problems began when I was in the army as a tank mechanic. I had to sit on cold steel to do my work.

After I got into getting fucked, problems were caused by short cocks that sort of jabbed at the deep cleft to my hole. There were tears created by people sticking a finger in my hole with long fingernails. Stress at work, from my family or lover, would create diarrhea that tore at my hole. Clap and amoebas took their toll as well. I have not had one problem with my asshole for over four years. I attribute this good fortune to handballing, being free of disease, and letting stressful situations dissolve. I have trained my asshole and myself.

The sphincter muscle has only two other muscles like it in the whole body: the eye muscles that cause you to wink. The sphincter can be very delicate. It can also be very resilient.

Just inside the sphincter is the prostate, where the seminal fluid is stored after the testes produce it. In and around that are the perineum muscles which pump blood into the cock. The blood is stored in a pocket beside these muscles. This pocket of blood can be hemorrhaged very easily, and is the reason that handballing can be very dangerous. People can bleed to death very quickly if this pocket is ruptured.

The anal canal is a mucous membrane that is also very resilient and can be stretched and trained just as the sphincter can be trained. This membrane, if scratched while it is stretched, can pop and tear just as a balloon can be popped; therefore it can be a very dangerous area.

With all this danger in handballing, it is not to be attempted by people who haven't trained themselves. Climbing mountains is dangerous, but not impossible. So is handballing. You have to have the knowledge and the tools to do both.

Handballing can be done with surgical gloves if that is your choice, but there is a case for gloveless handballing as well. I think that tactile response should remain intact for penetrational handballing. With the danger that is involved, this response is crucial for sensible handballing. If one squeezes a lime on his finger tips, the stinging pain from an opening in the skin will tell him where not to use that hand. In handballing, if there is no opening in the skin, there is no way that disease can be transmitted from one to the other. There can be no fluid contacts with handballing when done properly.

Some people, from the standpoint of disease transmission, feel safer using gloves. With gloves, the fingernail ends are smoother and trauma from sharp nails is reduced. It is a matter of choice and common sense.

Sixty-nine handballing, with both men playing bottom and top at the same time, can be very dangerous as there is grease everywhere. If this kind of session is attempted, be neat and have everything "at hand", so to speak: separate towels and lubricants, a bottle of alcohol for quick antiseptic use, an extra supply of gloves, and so forth. Also, keep the using hand only on or in the other person's body and off your body. That will help to keep your fluids your own. Clean yourselves immediately upon the consummation of the act. Two bottoms playing together can be fraught with danger. Since this is my forte I am very careful.

I once suggested sixty-nine to a friend. He said, "No, it is much too dangerous." When he is asked, "What do you do?" he replies, "Oh. . .I'm a bottom." He only looks for tops. I suspect this to be the real reason. He is very right about not wanting to play with another bottom. Since he is antibody negative it must work for him.

Before handballing the anal canal must be cleaned of all debris. As with all ass-play, the douche should be two to three hours before the ass-play is to begin. Remember to use the aloe vera before and after ass-play.

Many people who are into handballing use their eyes for communication. I try to guide the top when I'm on the bottom. When I'm the top, I question him about the progress. Communication is very important.

I never handball with anyone who doesn't get handballed. I want experienced people in my hole for this kind of action. If he doesn't have a red hanky in his right pocket I don't go with him. It's as simple as that. There are those who pontificate in their ivory towers about the dangers of handballing who have never had a finger up their butt.

I have experience and the experiences of others to draw upon. I have only known one person who went to the hospital. He asked for it, was suicidal about it, and had a partner who was known to be dangerous. That was very attractive to him.

It's not what you do, where you do it, who you do it with. It's not when you do it, nor why you do it, it's how well you do it. Handballing, I believe, can be a sensible activity.

In preparing for sex, the playroom and toys should be made as hygienic as an operating room. Give yourself plenty of time to accomplish this. Toys should be sprayed with a germicide or, as a much cheaper alternative, soaked in a solution of household bleach (hydrogen chloride) and water in a ratio of six parts water to one part bleach. As far as efficacy is concerned, there is nothing better than bleach.

Let the toys air dry, preferably in the sun. Warming the toys in a microwave or a dishwasher—be careful you could reduce latex toys to lumps—is better than warming them in water. Moisture and warmth breed germs. This includes leather toys, straps and wraps. Sustained temperatures around 140 degrees, alcohol, hydrogen peroxide, bleach, and other commercial germicides definitely kill all harmful germs when properly applied.

Wash all linen in the bleach or germicide solutions. You might want to add the detergent used in most dishwashers to rid the linen of grease and the rancid smell of old grease. An alternative to linens is disposable paper towels.

There are a multitude of other brand names of disposable towels that are moistened with a solution that contains nonoxynol 9. Use them to wipe off the dildo just before insertion, or the condom-covered cock before insertion, or any number of other things to be inserted into the body. This is simply another precaution. These products are found in almost every market and drug store.

Keep a plastic bag-lined trash can in the play area or a supermarket paper bag that can be thrown out. When drying linen expose them for longer than necessary to dry them in the dryer or outdoors. Excessive heat and ultra-violet light destroy germs.

It is my choice, but also I believe it to be prudent to keep myself as germ free as possible, so I use a barber's hair clipper to clip short all my body hair. Every three months, on the solstice or equinox, I go through a ritual in which I clip my body hair until my body is well groomed.

I like hairy men as much as anybody, but even more, now I like to take out my clippers when I take on a hirsute man for the evening. I turn it into a ritual of sacrifice. If he can get into it, you can have yourself a good time. If nothing else, don't tell him until after you put the cuffs on him.

If the toys are old, have wires in them, or have sharp cutting edges that may draw blood, throw them out. Buy safe new toys. We all have disposable income; dispose of it in the drug store, the leather store, or "pleasure" store near you.

It once could be said that "Richard Locke is a cheap fuck."

Not anymore. I spent forty bucks on my last trip to the drug store. There are no more cheap fucks. Cheap fucks, sleaze, dark orgy rooms, long fingernails, and any number of other things from the past are, in the words of Margaret Mitchell, "gone with the wind."

We can all be AIDS preventive by proper nutrition and vitamin supplements, with proper hygiene in our daily as well as our sexual lives, with plenty of rest and exercise. Even so, the healthiest of bodies can be infected with this dread disease and succumb. Therefore it is best not to become infected as well as keeping a healthy body. It always comes back to *disease interruptus.*

Hank, the horny truck driver, a character I play in the Gage film *L.A. Tool & Die*, was fond of sport fucking. Wylie, the character I play opposite, didn't quite know what Hank was all about till he joined Hank in the Land Office tearoom. Sport fucking is for the fun of it. I believe in sport fucking, and I believe most of my readers enjoy it as well.

Like other sports, we only compete with ourselves. There is no cheating involved. It's sportsmanship of the higher order. These activities are much like the body builder who pumps iron to create the body he wants. Arnold Schwarzenegger likens pumping iron to orgasm. You can get cock-hard listening to him talk about it.

I have never fucked with anybody that I didn't love. It may have been for only five minutes, but I loved him and still do. I have shot all over a thousand men who came to see me play with them. With all the live shows I have done (two and three shows a day) and all the men, and sometimes women, who have seen my show, I may have fucked with more people than anyone on the planet. I loved every one of them.

If there is a philosophy of sex, then I think I have a handle on part of what it is all about, and I have tried to share it with as many people as possible. Pride in oneself and the people you're with is the foundation of that philosophy. Trust is also very basic to sex. The heart and core is love. When you have pride, trust, and love, you have it made.

A Los Angeles gay newspaper publishes a safe sex checklist of twenty-one items. Of those twenty-one items, three are things you can do sexually and six are what you can't do sexually. The other do's and don'ts have to do with lifestyle. At the top of the list is: "Do have sex with the same partner." If I had only had sex with my late lover, I'd be dead. He would have pumped me full of AIDS every time we hit the sack.

At the top of the don't list is: "Don't have sex with many partners." If I have cut my sex partners from twenty a week to only five and one of the five has twenty partners a week, what have I gained? Absolutely nothing. It is not who you do—it's how you do it.

Sport fucking with many different partners exposes one to repeated infection of not only AIDS but all the other sexually transmitted diseases. It is prudent, then, to protect yourself and those you contact. Anything else is irresponsible, selfish, deadly behavior. It's not sport fucking in any sense. As a sport fucker, when you encounter irresponsible behavior, it is your duty to yourself, to him, and to your fellow man to put a stop to it. Sport fucking, in a responsible manner, is what I call modified polygamy. ▼

❖ ❖ ❖ ❖ ❖ ❖
NEW
YORK
JACKS
❖ ❖ ❖ ❖ ❖ ❖

New
York
Jacks

❖ ❖ ❖ ❖ ❖

Hot men standing in shadows, cocks in their hands, lights playing across their crotches, stroking themselves, across, down and up the shafts of their cocks—this is one of the most beautiful experiences we can have: The body and soul of a man bared for his fellows. His body responding to his own caress. His legs splayed out in front of him, the stringy muscles of his calves and thighs standing out from the bulkier muscles that bunch under the strain of his whole body arching up and into his hand. His stomach washboarded into neat rows and mounds of hard muscles. His arms stretched to his cock as he strokes with one hand, holding his balls with the other. His face revealing the severe bliss that only he can give to himself, engulfed from head to toe with the sensuousness of his own being.

Most men have contained their jerkoff fantasies in their own private worlds, and except for tenuous circle jerks ninety-nine per cent of most jerking is singular, private, and alone. However, I have seen multiple jerkoffs countless times in my travels with my road show across the country. Many times.

Many men, together, jerking themselves off for each other's pleasure, each one physically, emotionally, and spiritually different in the expression of the beast in him. Yet these jerkoffs all have a few things in common. Only they themselves know how and where their passion is flashed. They alone know the intricacies of the triggers that will inflame their bodies.

I first viewed the phenomenon in 1978 in San Francisco. A friend invited me to his home. He had removed all the furniture and put down wrestling mats everywhere but the bedroom. We all jerked off wherever and with whomever we decided. The only rule was that it had to be jerkoff. At the end of the evening, we all sat in one room on the floor and had a circle jerk. It was all very informal.

Jerkoff clubs, to my knowledge, have been around for many years. The meetings I have attended are for people who are not necessarily exhibitionists or voyeurs. They provide a place for men to "come" together, to compare notes, bodies, cocks, to watch, to learn. One can appraise techniques as well as exhibit oneself to others.

In New York City, one night in October, 1980, I attended a meeting of the New York Jacks at the invitation of Joe Gage, the director of most of my better movies. The Jacks met in a bar on Christopher Street, and the first time I walked into the place, I realized it was the epitome of the bars I had always visualized in my fantasies. The door was open at nine and closed at nine-thirty, and it remained closed till midnight. No one was allowed in or out. Clothes were checked, even your pants, so one shouldn't take valuables with him. After you check your clothes, you just turn toward the bar and there you are.

Men, men standing singly, men in groups of two, three or more, talking and playing with themselves and each other.

Jacks wearing jockstraps, in shorts, or standing there nude, stroking themselves. At first the action seems slow, for everyone is waiting until they are locked in. Gradually they drift into the backroom where the action begins.

The Jacks are all ages and sizes: tall, short, stocky, lean. Their cocks run the gamut as well: long, short, thick and thin. They are all unabashed about why they are here. The Jacks are purists. There is no assplay. There is no cocksucking. Just jerkoff. The rule is not to be violated. The members will allow casual forbidden play for only a moment, but if one Jack won't say anything, another one will. Everyone is courteous and no one forces his attention where it is not wanted. This particular attitude is what attracts me.

Many times, I have wanted to be a participant in a scene in an orgy room without having to become a part of the action, to stroke my cock as an observer. Since I'm always the entertainer, I never get to see a show for myself. I, too, like to be entertained. In the rarefied atmosphere of the New York Jacks, I can watch men perform for me, doing what they do best, jerking off.

The Jacks have been around for some time, and although the club was fairly popular in the "good old days," the current health crisis has made membership grow. Growth might kill the easy atmosphere, but the Jacks' integrity will remain.

I received my membership card in the summer of 1983, and became a member in one of the best men's clubs in the world, the New York Jacks. I had to be sponsored for three visits before I was eligible for membership. I was so excited about my first visit as a member that I have not only recorded it indelibly in my mind, but also in my sex diary. The following is the entry of my visit of June 11, 1983; coincidentally, that was the celebration of my birthday:

The New York Jacks meet on every Tuesday and every

other Thursday. I arrived early that night to permit my voyeurism full rein. I sat down and had a beer and shared a joint with a friend. We talked about my current visit to New York City and my work with various AIDS projects. I began to grope myself while watching the arrival of the cocksmen. Everybody loves a parade.

After a time, I excused myself and went to the winding circular staircase. Through the iron bars, I could see the Jacks pulling their cocks, eyeing each other, as I climbed toward them. All eyes were leveled at crotches. Completely engrossed in each other, the Jacks didn't see me. My cock was already up and hard in my jockstrap. I pulled my cock out and watched for a few minutes before I entered the circle.

I remembered one of the Jacks from my first visit. He has one of the largest cocks of the group. With a bit of an upturn, it was thick and full and stood straight out from his body. There were jars of Albolene everywhere, and I put some on my cock and began stroking. Noticing my arrival, a Jack next to me turned to give me a better view as well as entrance to the circle. I glanced up from the crotches surrounding me to see the room filling slowly but steadily with Jacks. There was very little talking and what little there was got me harder.

"Pull it, buddy."

"Yeah, yeah, fucker, pull that beautiful cock."

"Hey, man, let me grab it? Let me have it? Ah, fuck, man, you've got a cock. Let me have it?"

There were moans and groans as the Jacks brought themselves closer and closer to coming, then they would back down. It was like a rollercoaster with each rider in a different car, on the downhill and uphill slopes of the structure.

The Jack with the big cock reached into his sock and pulled out a popper which he snapped into my face. I took a big hit. I had to bring myself down—the rigid cock in my hand was pulsing with the throb of my heart. It pumped more blood into my cock as the vessels dilated. I let my cock go and felt it throbbing. I breathed in the smell of these men, I moaned in their heat, I felt the charge of sexual energy generated by the circle. The circle enveloped all time and space. Nothing had ever happened before, nothing would ever again; it was all now.

The Jack who had pleaded for the beautiful cock finally won his prize. He reached to the man's thigh and grabbed hold. He had his buddy's cock in his hand. His buddy threw back his head and flung his arms in the air.

He grabbed at the man's hand and said, "No, fucker, not yet. No...no, I'm going to come! Fucker, don't! Oooh...you son of a bitch."

The Jacks tightened the circle, hands from out of nowhere began caressing his backside. A hand proffered a popper, another squeezed his tit. His hands, outstretched over his head, almost in prayer primordial, were quivering, his fingers extended.

"I'm coming. Oh, God, I'm coming!"

The Jacks in the circle began to chant with him.

"Yeah. Buddy. Come. Fucker."

"Shoot it to us...ohhh, yeah!"

"Hey Jack, do it!"

"Come, shoot it, come on, buddy...jack his cock. Make him feel it."

"Hey, yeah, feel it. Feel my hand stroking your cock. Yeah, buddy, spurt in my hand, buddy. Yeah, that's it. Ohhh...give it to me...oh, yeah."

From all around, the Jack got his support. We were all pulling with his buddy and felt, with him, the cum rise in our balls. Our crotches spasmed. The muscles between our balls and our assholes throbbed. This would be the first of the evening; he shot. The hand stroking his cock withdrew, so we could all see the cock arch to his stomach with each spurt. It shot out into the air and onto the floor except for that cum that was stringing down the leg of the buddy who had stroked it out of this Jack. He didn't seem to notice it.

While the Jack shot his wad, the rest of us brought our cocks back from the brink of ejaculation. We wanted the "Valley of Orgasm"—all of us except my buddy with the big cock. He had gone too far, had lost his control. He couldn't, and at this point wouldn't, stop the cum from gushing out of his cock. Now the first Jack, he too was coming. The first comer had grabbed his own cock again. He stroked the last drops from his cock, picking up the tempo of his stroke as he watched the big cock coming. The first Jack came again. A buddy can stroke the cum out of you, but not all of it. There is still more in the reservoir waiting for the touch only you know how to give yourself to totally drain the cum from your body. After coming twice, the first Jack's body was radiant from cum while the big cock continued to shoot.

Another guy was already coming in a nearby group as I joined them. The Jack across from him was coming, too. I had my cock pretty well along, so I reached out and grabbed the balls next to me. Their owner was pleased to have me lend a hand. He reciprocated. We pulled each other's balls, building the pressure in our groins as we each stroked our own cocks.

The "Valley of Orgasm" was going to have to wait. This was going to be the first cum shot of the evening for all of us. With a long night ahead of us, it's best to get rid of it, so we can go longer later.

A Jack watching us from across the circle began to come. The peak was near for all of us. I let out a hard breath and began to moan loudly. The rest of the circle was in the same state of arousal, and we began to come together, our eyes flicking back and forth across the circle, trying to catch it all. Around the circle, cocks were ejecting cum all over the floor and on one of the legs of a Jack who deliberately stood in the way. It was hot. I was hot. And it was only ten o'clock. "Oh, what a night!"

The rules are simple, seven in all, but the last is the most important. "Relax and enjoy yourself: We're all friendly and horny." The rest of the rules are basically behavioral. Activity is strictly J/O. No oral or anal sex or ass play permitted. No piss scenes. Street clothes, including pants, must be checked on entering. Each member is responsible for his guest's behavior all evening. I don't believe there is any policy concerning membership except that of being of the male gender.

I never enjoyed being a member of anything. I never joined the Boy Scouts, although I hear that was a mistake. I never joined a political club, nothing. I'm proud to say I'm a member in good standing of the New York Jacks, the San Francisco Jacks, and the Onanists of America. I'm as proud of my membership as anything I have ever done.

In a recent newsletter to the membership, there was comment about a person who allowed his guest to indulge in inappropriate behavior. The member explained his guest's behavior by saying, "I didn't know you were serious about those rules." Here is the reply from the New York Jacks representative:

"Our seriousness stems not from attempting to prevent transmission of disease, though hopefully that may be a fortuitous side effect, but from a positive, independently established desire to express ourselves through the medium of the group J/O."

I repeat this for you, dear reader, because it's the ground rule for the formation of any club of this type. I recommend joining, or forming a club, to anybody and everybody. Go to it, fellas.

Just remember to invite me when I'm in town. ▼

❖ ❖ ❖ ❖ ❖ ❖

THE
VALLEY OF
ORGASM

❖ ❖ ❖ ❖ ❖ ❖

The
Valley of
Orgasm

❖ ❖ ❖ ❖ ❖

This essay delves into an area that I am beginning to explore more thoroughly. During the years when I was touring the country with my stage show, I would prepare for my performance about a half-hour prior to my entrance by taking 1600 units of vitamin E and a candy bar while bringing myself close to orgasm and holding there. By the time I got onto the stage, I was near the peak of sexual exhilaration and holding until the sound cue, usually a blast of thunder, and then shoot into the third row. These experiences (as well as the fisting I have experienced for the last five years) have brought me into the "Valley of Orgasm" many times.

One day while I was walking up Castro Street, feeling very ineffective in the face of all the madness of our times and lost in deep thought, a man appeared right in my face, very suddenly.

He introduced himself to me as Joe Kramer, of the "Body Electric," a massage studio in Berkeley. It was magic. We both had a lot in common. Sometimes people come into our lives when they are most needed and not until then. Joe was a godsend. Many times, while performing my stage show, the "Valley of Orgasm" was with me. I had never thought about or realized there was such a thing, even though I had experienced it many times. Joe began to relate to me his experiences in what he calls ecstatic sex. Subsequently, we formed a very special relationship and taught a class together in "Ecstatic, Sensible Sex." Then I received the following letter:

I appreciate your latest series of articles on sensible sex. I have felt that the concept of an actual published manual for both straights and gays on sensible sex techniques would be very marketable and profitable.

My personal, major, sensible sex technique is simple: monogamy. Simple but shattering. I had to let go of my personal self-imagery as a lone sex-cub playfully prowling and get down to the real possibility that one man can satisfy and love me. It has been quite a growing-up experience. Perhaps not a technique for all, but it's been the major one that has changed my life and its quality. AIDS awareness moved me into my heart and out of my cock.

The other "technique" that has made our sexual play revolutionary is Tantric Sex play: taking the energy about to burst from a cum-loaded dick and taking it "somewhere else." I lack the writer's ability to describe what happens, but I am filled with ecstasy and love, being with my partner. We call it the "valley" orgasm: going for sustaining the flow, the buzz, the rush, rather than the "peak" orgasm.

Coming now often feels just like one amongst other options concerning what to do with sexual energy—often an option that seems too easy and kind of "the same old thing," rather than the mystery of my body shaking uncontrollably, thick ropes of cum flowing from my cock without the spasms of ejaculation, the visions I see, the warm expansions I feel in my chest, the laughter and tears without reason.

Unfortunately, I never met any men who were willing and wanted to "go to those places" with me, but I'm sure they exist. Luckily, I now have someone who is more than willing to explore masculine/feminine sexual energy.

In closing, good luck to you and your work with the men out there who need your help and knowledge.

Ed K.

Since Joe has the expertise, I asked him to reply to this letter. This is what he said:

If you are interested in healthy and ecstatic ways to have sex in an epidemic, I recommend checking out an ancient Chinese approach: Taoism. While most male sex today is concerned with discharging erotic energy from the body, the Tao of sex suggests charging the body with sexual energy. Distinguishing between ejaculation and orgasm, a Taoist wants to enhance and prolong orgasm while not discharging the erotic energy from the body in ejaculation.

A good way to introduce yourself to this erotic experience is to masturbate for two hours or more without ejaculation. Within the first thirty minutes, you will begin to feel erotically charged. The longer you play with yourself, the lighter you will get. You can control the degree of charge by how close to ejaculation you stay. Remaining just below the point of ejaculation, inevitably for a long period, is what Taoists call valley orgasm, or riding the wave of bliss. I call it erotic surfing.

If you are not accustomed to marathon masturbation, let me suggest some hints to enhance your pleasure:

Wake up and stretch out your body before your two-hour session. Go for a run or take an aerobics class. The more alive your body is, the more you will feel.

Keep your body as relaxed as possible during the session. Trying to maintain an erection for two hours by tensing muscles will only produce cramps and exhaustion.

Pay attention to your body, rather than fantasizing. Taoist sex is a body experience rather than a head trip. Breathe fully and regularly. Constricting the breath helps some men intensify ejaculation, but the goal here is not to ejaculate. Subventilation numbs our body sensations.

Use lubricants on your penis. Dry rubbing for long periods of time can damage and numb nerve endings. Don't limit your self-erotic massage to your penis. Explore your body geography.

Move or shake your body as you get higher. Taoism approaches sex like a martial art. You are circulating erotic energy through your body. When that energy gets blocked or stuck, especially in the hips, you often lose control and ejaculate.

If you really wish to have a completely Taoist sexual experience, don't ejaculate at the end of the session. Pay close attention to your body for twenty-four hours after this experience.

This solo experiment is only an introduction to Taoism. Taoist techniques can be practiced alone, with another or in groups.

AIDS is a deadly disease. It does exist. It has physical properties. Someday there may be a cure. However, that day has not arrived.

AIDS is preventable. We know that. It is simply a matter of "how" we conduct ourselves. I caught hepatitis in 1970 in a monogamous relationship. Athletic, healthy, happy people have caught AIDS. A man I knew in New York was celibate for four months and threw himself off a building. One man told me that AIDS was caused by guilt; he had spent ten years in a seminary, so he must know what guilt is.

There is an "escape" from hysterical thinking. It's called sensible sex. Rather than mourning the old ways, I am looking forward to the new ways. Ways in which health, quality relationships, happiness, and a great deal of satisfaction are *de rigueur*. More and more, I'm finding that there really is nothing to mourn. A life that is free of disease is the present and future for me. ▼

❖ ❖ ❖ ❖ ❖ ❖

VOLUNTEER AT WARD 5B

❖ ❖ ❖ ❖ ❖ ❖

Volunteer
at Ward 5B

❖ ❖ ❖ ❖ ❖

The people on the ward think of themselves as People With AIDS and not AIDS Victims. This thinking permeates the ward. For the most part these people are very cheerful, considering that sometimes in each and every room could be a person very critically ill and near to death.

I met Jay Allen on the day I went for the required medical tests for all the volunteers at San Francisco General Hospital. My volunteer specialty is massage. While Jay and I were waiting for the tests to begin, I found out that Jay's specialty was trimming and styling hair and that we were both volunteering for the AIDS Ward on 5B. He and I worked together off and on for about a year before he became ill. He committed suicide soon after his diagnosis. The pain of his disease and, I suppose, of living was too great.

As I worked on the ward, I came into contact with many volunteers from many areas.

There were the Shanti Volunteers whose specialty with the terminally ill was to make the transition as easy as possible. Shanti does everything from arranging housing upon release from the hospital to counseling for the bereaved. Jessie McVey, one of those little old ladies that you often hear about, is a Shanti Volunteer and is always there taking care of minor emergencies, assisting the nurse or another Shanti volunteer, or holding the hand of the mother as they sit in silence awaiting the report of the doctor.

The chaplain's office recruited more clergy for the increased burden that Ward 5B placed on the hospital's staff. Among them was the jovial Ed Barns. Especially at Christmas time, the presence of Ed was seen everywhere. From rolling the piano from the seventh floor to the Ward 5B hallway for an impromptu or special Christmas choral tribute (in which he himself would sing a rich baritone carol), to simply holding the hand of a volunteer whose grief had become overwhelming, to stomping and bellowing demands that a person with AIDS deserved better treatment from his family. Ed stands out in my mind because of how great a person he is. There are more than just he on the chaplain's staff, and all are just as great as Ed. Such a crew of dedicated people seems not easy to find, yet there they are.

In the early days of my volunteering on the ward, I spent many hours massaging only the feet of People With AIDS. I have been a masseur for over fifteen years and I am licensed and certified by the state of California. When a patient's arms are needled and hosed up to bags of medicines, it is not easy to give a good, overall massage. It is best to simply massage the feet. Since one-sixteenth of the body's number of muscles are located in the feet, there is a direct correlation of foot massage to pleasure. As well, one form of foot massage, Reflexology, purports to heal the entire body from the connections of nerves in the muscles of the feet.

I would walk into the room and come close to the person in the bed, hold his feet as I introduced myself, and ask if he would like a massage. Very few have ever declined. When they do, I persist for only a few moments. Their privacy must never be violated, but at the same time their first moments in their realization that they have just been diagnosed with a terminal disease is very unsettling, and in their helplessness, they are often afraid to reach out.

A person who volunteers on the ward becomes many things to many people when he walks into a room not knowing just what to expect. It isn't easy for them or for you. They are embarrassed to be put into the position of having someone else do things for them. Simple things such as bowel movements become a matter for two, as do trimming nails, eating, answering the phone, and any number of other things. After some time, the embarrassment experienced by you and the patient is overcome. And then you settle into a comfortable place with him and yourself.

The ward only has volunteers. The nursing staff, the medical staff, the support workers in the janitorial and culinary fields, the movie stars such as Elizabeth Taylor and politicians like Pete Wilson, all volunteer to walk onto the ward. These people have seen the courage to face the future when the future may be very soon to die away. The courage is a halo around the ward and all who pass through those portals are intensely aware of it.

The nursing staff, in the beginning, was led by Cliff Morrison, the pioneer who guided the ward through many crises. Our first meeting was a bust. Prior to my arriving at the nurses' station, a fanatic had run onto the ward throwing Christian literature and yelling, "Repent, sinners." My appearance shortly afterward put them off; the ward was closed to strangers.

The AIDS ward gets assaulted from all sides. Ward 5B was a grand experiment not totally acceptable to many. Representative Dannemeyer has kept up a constant barrage of hate and animosity towards the ward. He once complained of the X-rated videos available to the people on the ward—the ones I had donated. They were returned to me post haste after

Dannemeyer went public about them.

Many politicians are miffed at the mollycoddling of AIDS patients on the ward. My observation is that to coddle as much as one can is never enough. In the meantime, Dannemeyer has attacked the hospital itself—with the help of five nurses who felt that extra care, gloves, and masks should be the choice of the worker. The ward argued back that the precautions were unnecessary and the sight of suited care givers would cause psychological impairment to the patient. Uncalled-for precautions would damage patient well-being, and the resulting despair could cause early death.

We have come a long way. Ward 5A, the new and larger AIDS ward, is the offspring of Cliff Morrison's ingenuity and far-sightedness. A man ahead of his time. Ward 5A is run today by Allison Moed. There are not enough words to express the dynamics of this woman. The gay community should be very happy with this "straight" sister who has voluntarily come to us. She needs no award for what she does, but wouldn't it be nice for the federal government to give her the highest civilian award it can give. Give it to her; she deserves more.

She zealously guards "The Book," a record filled with the names and the dates of the deaths of those who visited the ward. A book of memories, photos of the parties, the gay weddings (I attended two), Christmas photos, obituaries in the gay newspapers—memorabilia of all kinds wedged into the pages.

My gay "brother" (lover), Allen, is recorded in this book. He died on June 21, 1984. One of the reasons I became a volunteer was to repay the kindnesses shown him. His mother related to me how she was given a place to shower in the doctors' quarters, so that she never left his bedside for more than a few moments. She felt the staff had treated her as a queen. Allen had spent two weeks in intensive care before he died.

I began my massage visits on Sundays. Sunday was my day off, and the parking is much easier on Sunday. The families come on Sundays, and Sundays are usually a party occasion. Every other Sunday for over three years, Rita Rocket has brought her "Brunch Bunch." Most of the time, the Brunch Bunch is good, home-cooked delicious food served up by Rita and her waiters. Over the years, they have included Bobby, Terry, Tony, Chuck, and then there's Johnny, who makes and serves the desserts. There are none like his desserts; whether it's a fruit tart or chocolate mousse or chocolate covered strawberries, this is the finest food served in any hospital.

Rita and I met one Sunday at a bar. She was dancing on the pool table and raising money for her Brunch Bunch. I told her I was doing massage on the ward, and she invited me to be a waiter for her. On our first day together Rita swooped into a room and said, "Hi, I'm Rita Rocket—I'm your cheerleader for the day." Soon I began to help her set up and became her "star" waiter.

Rita and I, the Shanti volunteers and all the others on the ward produced a video, *In the Midst of Life*. This video can be found in hospitals from San Francisco to Copenhagen and is used to acquaint people with the safety of working in an "AIDS Ward." *In the Midst of Life* is the definitive training manual for giving "care" in hospitals to people with AIDS.

The cameras only recorded what occurred the days that they were there videotaping; the daily happenings on the AIDS ward are constantly changing. New arrivals pass those who have weathered the storm and are going home. Many make the transition, but are not removed until the quiet of the night.

On one of my first visits to the ward, I was halfway across the room when I realized that I was becoming more and more shocked. As I got closer to the person on the bed, I could see that all the flesh outside of the bed coverings was purpled and splotched with hardly a bit of normal skin showing. This was my first time under fire. I pulled my senses about me and kept my tears and my emotions and my love for him to myself. I kept from pouring out my soul to him. He didn't have to spend the time he had left with my tears. I introduced myself and asked if he would like a massage. By this time in his journey, there wasn't much left of his body that didn't have pain. I sat and held his hand a few moments and left quietly. He died that night.

Another man had been in intensive care for over two months. His mouth had been opened to his lungs and a pipe shoved in to keep the air passage clear, with the pipe hooked to an oxygen machine. He had become better, but the end was not far off. He came out of intensive care and into the ward for a day before his move to Garden Sullivan, a hospital type of hospice. I came in and was told by the attending nurse that he couldn't talk. His mouth and throat were very sore from the machine. As I talked with the man, I began to uncover his feet and bring them into position for massage. I looked into his eyes and saw the smile of his eyes as I bent to my work.

Many people with AIDS are subject to fungal infections. One infection concerns the toenails. Nail bed fungus is found in about one-fourth of the People With AIDS. This gentleperson's feet were eaten up with fungus, despite all the wonderful care he received in intensive care. His upper body was very well bathed, but his feet had not been touched. Nail cutting is considered to be surgery and can only be done by a doctor. The toenails were half an inch thick and much too long. His feet were crusted with dead skin. I went to the sink and grabbed many towels and a basin with hot water. Since he couldn't sit up and soak his feet in a sitting position I wrapped his feet in hot wet towels and bathed his feet and cared for them as best I could. As I was finishing with a final touch of lotion to his feet, I glanced up and saw the tears flowing from those beautiful eyes. He knew his days were numbered. He couldn't move, he couldn't talk, and no one had noticed the condition of his feet. He, I'm sure, in embarrassment had never asked that his feet be bathed too when the staff had given him his bath. Intensive care is just that. All the machines have to be monitored, adjusted, turned on, and turned off, and there are constant little emergencies and buzzers and flashing lights—and too many patients and not enough nurses or volunteers to do a proper job of it. Every hospital everywhere is understaffed on all its wards and there isn't enough money.

Families come to the ward, sometimes for their last visits to a member of the family. Mothers and fathers, sisters and brothers, wives, daughters, and sons—and for the first time find out that their son is gay and that he has AIDS. Life decisions suddenly have to be made. Who is to make them? What is legal? What is not? What is experimental? Who gives permission? Sudden immersions into life-making decisions stress the emotional stabilities to the limits.

There are occasional groans of anguish that flutter through the ward. At other times there are myriads of laughter coming from rooms when one or another occupant flits hither and yon through the ward, wearing brocaded silk kimonos with kites and balloons and crepe trailing behind, and sharing his birthday cake, making sure that everyone receives a piece of what may be his last birthday cake. Life on the ward goes on day by day. Death is a passing shadow that floats through, more than just occasionally.

There are other volunteers such as the "Golden Arches" who come on Saturdays with home cooked food by a number of hairdressers who buy, cook, and serve the food. There is "The Godfather Fund"—volunteers who come by and hand out slippers, robes, stuffed animals, razors, and whatever.

There are so many volunteers that I have left out. Many I don't know, many who come in the quiet of night, many in the bustle of day. And there are many more at other hospitals in the city. I have met dozens and hundreds of volunteers.

I was in the first group of people to be trained by the Red Cross in New York City in June, 1983. Even though only one-tenth of the money given to the Red Cross eventually reaches the hands of the people victimized by flood, earthquake, or disease, the other nine-tenths to programs such as this one. A "Caregiver" teaches other "Caregivers" how to care for a person with AIDS: the proper hygienic way to bathe the person, the way to roll him into a new position, or to put him into a wheelchair. Give generously to the Red Cross. They make each penny and tenth of a penny count. They put the penny to its best use.

There are and have been hundreds and thousands of volunteers to help people with AIDS. We are more than just candy stripers or nurses in training. We are concerned. We come from all walks of life. We are old. We are young. We are hairdressers and construction workers. We are mothers, we are fathers, daughters and sons. Unfortunately, we are not enough. There is not enough money, not enough hospital beds, not enough of anything. We can find a place for all volunteers whether it's in education at the AIDS Hotline or massaging feet, or simply holding a hand. We need you. An hour a week by a million people is a million hours. That's about 46,000 days, or nearly a hundred years of care. The reward often times is only a tear or a thank you. ▼

❖ ❖ ❖ ❖ ❖ ❖

INTERVIEW

❖ ❖ ❖ ❖ ❖ ❖

Interview

❖ ❖ ❖ ❖ ❖

The following interview was taped in Guerneville, California on January 21, 1992 by Jerry Douglas, and appeared in the December 1992 issue of Manshots *magazine.*

The chinstrap beard is a bit grayer and the crow's feet a tad more pronounced, but otherwise, Richard Locke looks very much the same as he did at the peak of his popularity in the late seventies and early eighties. He stands on the deck of the summer house he has leased in Russian River country for the winter. He is wearing jeans and a flannel shirt, smoking a cigarette, and flashing his unique smile as he waves a welcome. We have not seen each other for many years, but we pick up right where we left off, and spend the day wandering the woodsy gay resort area, strolling along the riverbank itself, driving to nearby Bodega Bay for lunch, and returning to his temporary home to sit in front of a wood burning fireplace well into the evening. And most of the time, the tape recorder is whirring away.

Manshots: Well, what have you been doing since the last time you were seen onscreen?

Locke: Actually, I did some safe sex seminars, and also some live shows since I've been on the screen. My last film was *Daddy Dearest*. I made it in 1983 in New York with Artie Bressan. But I did a lot of stage shows—opened the Campus Theatre in San Francisco, and on their first anniversary, I did a safe sex seminar.

Manshots: How's your sex life these days?

Locke: Well, I have the virus in my body, so I don't kiss much anymore, unless I know the person very well. Like my lover.

Manshots: You've long been in the forefront of the AIDS wars. Do you remember the first time you heard about AIDS?

Locke: Yeah. I remember it was in 1982—they called it the gay cancer then.

Manshots: Did the spectre of AIDS have anything to do with your decision to stop making films?

Locke: Well, I felt that there were more important things to do. I read Larry Kramer's article, "1, 112 and Counting," and the whole thrust of the thing was: We are in the middle of an epidemic and nobody's doing anything. I went home and sat on a rock, and I thought about it, and I said, "Well, Richard, you're somebody who is a somebody, and what are you doing?" So I went back to New York and stayed with a friend who was working with the AIDS Research Center at the time—and basically, I retired from the screen and stage— to use my name to try and influence young kids.

Manshots: What was the first thing you were able to do?

Locke: I took a course from the American Red Cross on how to take care of people with AIDS. It was the first course they gave. And I took a course from the GMHC on crisis intervention. So, really, the first thing I did was to make myself knowledgeable. The course I took from the Red Cross—in hygiene—made me realize there was so much I'd thrown out the window when I started licking assholes. Y'know, when you're licking an asshole, you don't think about hygiene. Well, taking this course, I just re-learned a lot of stuff and re-incorporated it. And it's good common sense—that's why I call it, not safe sex, but sensible sex. So that's when I started formulating my own sensible sex techniques. I went back to the desert, after spending six, seven months in New York finding out what was going on, educating myself. Then I started trying to get Palm Springs interested in developing some kind of organization like the GMHC, but they weren't interested. Right about that same time, my lover died. I left the desert and went to San Francisco to do what I could —which wasn't very easy. My whole life has been in the desert.

Manshots: Let's talk about that. Joe Gage described you as a desert rat.

Locke: Oh, yeah, I certainly was. There are a lot of reasons why I love the desert. One is because it has fewer people in it, and I see the big problem confronting the world today as overpopulation. There are too many people consuming too many things and leaving their wastes. I've always been interested in the twenty-first century. So what I was doing in the desert was trying to build a twenty-first century house. I built this geodesic dome. One person can build it, I thought. But it takes more than one person, because of the lattice construction—someone has to hold one end while you're bolting the other. So I was wrong about that. I wanted a do-it-yourself project. My whole thinking is that Prince Charming is not going to come along and save your ass. If you're going to be happy, you're going to be happy within and of yourself, 'cause happiness doesn't come with Prince Charming.

Manshots: You're probably one of the most self-sufficient men I've ever known, and yet, you've always had a lover or been in tandem with another person.

Locke: Well, I really feel it's a do-it-yourself world. You've gotta do it yourself. If you're happy, then you're going to attract happiness, and be able to share it. But if you're looking for happiness, desperately, you're not going to find it. So I wanted a house to build myself—but I realized that you've got to have someone else to hold the other end of the board. What you have to do is select people and be wise in your selection. I'm lucky. I've had some wonderful people in my life. Many of them are gone now. I still have a few. If I have any regrets at all in my life, my one regret is that I didn't make more straight friends, more women friends, because at one point I was desolate. All my friends were dead. I ran in the fast lane; people I knew all over the country were running in the fast lane, too. My good, best friends are all dead. I've had to make new friends, and I've been wise in my later years by making friends of women, straight friends. Because I know they will still be around to remember me after I'm gone.

Manshots: Richard, a great many people will remember you.

Locke: Y'know, I have a whole stack of fan letters, but one really sticks out in my mind—from Ypsilanti, Michigan. This guy told me he drove five, six hours to a movie theatre to sit down and "for two hours, I could be myself." Then he had to go back to his wife and kids. That was very important to me, because what I was doing for him was living a life he couldn't live.

Manshots: You've always been up-front about whatever you do. For one thing, Richard Locke is your real name.

Locke: Yeah.

Manshots: I think you and I are the only two people in this business who use our own names.

Locke: Well, Wakefield Poole did, and there are a few others. But not many. I remember one of the first movies I made, they said, "What name do you want?" I said, "My name." And they said, "You don't want 'Myles Longue' or something like that?" And I said, "No, I'm very proud of my work and everything I do. An artist signs his name to the canvas, and I sign my name."

Manshots: What's the first movie you did?

Locke: *Dreamer*.

Manshots: How did that come about?

Locke: Well, I was sitting in the apartment of a friend of mine, just off Santa Monica Boulevard in L.A., and an acquaintance of ours came by. Well, he's sitting there, and he says, "Richard, I'm doing some casting for a friend of mine named Jim West. He's doing a film. Would you like to be in it?" I said, "Sure. "

Manshots: Had you ever thought about it before?

Locke: (*That crooked smile*) Oh, I'd thought about it a lot. Not porno films, but films. I took courses in film in college, and I realized that in order to make films in Hollywood, you had to (1) have money, (2) know somebody, or (3) be in the union. And I was none of that, so I gave it all up. Five years later, I'm in Hollywood, and this guy says, "You want to be in a movie?" He adds, "It's porno." I say, "Great—that's my two favorite hobbies, combined." And I know, if I ever write an autobiography—which I've considered—I have several titles. One is *I Didn't Say No*, another is *I Said Yes*, and another one is *I Didn't Do It for the Money*. I remember Al Parker saying, one time, "The difference between being famous and infamous is that one has money." And it's true. There's no money in the porno business for the artists.

Manshots: When did you meet Jim West for the first time?

Locke: Well, when I told this guy yes, he said, "I'll set you up with Jim." So I met Jim, and he said, "Well, we're going to San Diego." *Dreamer*'s all about this guy who sees these different people and dreams about them. And I said, "Why don't you call it *Dreamer*?" So. (*A pause*) I had a lot to do with that film besides being in it. Same thing happened on *Cruising the Castro*. We went out to make a film at the beach, and it was raining. I didn't want to lose out on the shoot. I needed the money. So I said, "Why don't we do a film called *Cruising the Castro*? And start right here on Castro Street." And the guy who was making the film had a flat on Castro, so I gave him the subplot, and I did my third, and that's when I met Will Seagers—though I knew him at that point under his real name. In fact, Joe Gage was real pissed off when he heard I was making a film with Will. I didn't know he was the same guy who was going to be my partner in *L.A. Tool & Die*. So we made a film together before *L.A.*, and Joe was pissed.

Manshots: I've never seen *Cruising the Castro*.

Locke: I've never seen it. Another one of those films I've never seen. *Two Days in a Hot Place*, I've never seen. A few others. I lived out in the desert. And *Two Days in a Hot Place* was forgettable.

Manshots: When you walked on the set as a performer for the first time, how did you deal with the camera, the crew, the lights?

Locke: You know, I've been asked that question a lot. And what comes to mind right off the bat is that guy in Ypsilanti. Also, Gloria Swanson in *Sunset Boulevard*, when she talks about "those wonderful people out there in the dark." Well, I never did it for the camera. I always did it for those people out there on the other side of the camera. The camera was merely a tool to get me to the audience. So I always did it for the audience, and that's one reason I had no trouble getting it up. Deep in my heart, I'm a voyeur.

Manshots: More a voyeur than an exhibitionist?

Locke: More. And as a voyeur, I know what I like to see, and so all I have to do is flip myself on the screen as to what I'd want to see, as a voyeur. And still, I would rather watch. Y'know, I'd go into the orgy room at a bathhouse—I wanted to watch. I didn't want to be a part of it. And my stage shows. (*Chuckles*) I'm giving away my secrets now. I like to look at things in a historical perspective. So I go back in history and I look at Gypsy Rose Lee and the musical, *Gypsy*. They have a song in there, "You Gotta Have a Gimmick." I thought about it a lot—what is going to be my gimmick? So what I tried to do with my stage shows was I put a few props onstage—a dressing mirror, a coat rack, to try and simulate my bedroom. So the people in the audience are sitting there looking in my bedroom.

Manshots: They all become peeping Toms, then.

Locke: To make it come off right, you never pay attention to the people in the audience, you never give any one person your attention, because if you do, you break the spell. And also, everybody else gets pissed at you because you're playing to that one guy. So that was my gimmick—I played to an audience of voyeurs. I tried to give them what they wanted to see, and what I as a voyeur thought would be hot.

Manshots: When did you do your first stage show?

Locke: It was right after *El Paso*, I think. I got a call to go to Washington, D.C.

Manshots: What was your show like?

Locke: Here's another one of my gimmicks: to take the ordinary and mundane, and make it erotic. When I went to Washington, I took a business suit with me, and I stripped out of that suit into leather. Everybody in Washington has to wear a suit because they work in the government, so I took their "ordinary" and eroticized it. The last gimmick I have is to see to it my show has a beginning, a middle, and an end. I tried to tell a story, with every show I did. In this one, I am a businessman who has a date that night. I come home from work. I've been thinking about the date all day. I come out onstage. I get a hard-on. I'm in my bedroom with the mirror and coat rack. The coat rack has all my leather on it. I pull out my hard-on and start jerking off. I start stripping out of the business suit. The last thing I take off is the shirt. Underneath it is my harness, my leather harness. I've been wearing it all day in anticipation of this date tonight. I walk out to the edge of the stage, shoot all over the audience—on cue, on a sound cue! Then I go back, put on my leather. As I finish, you hear the sound of a motorcycle and a voice saying, "You ready, Richard?" I say, "Yeah" and go offstage as you hear the sound of another motorcycle start up. A beginning, a middle, and an end. A story. That's why I did a real sex show onstage—because I couldn't do less than what I'd done on film. And as far as I know, I was the first person to come—onstage—all across the country. I broke new ground.

Manshots: Let's talk about your remarkable professional partnership with Joe Gage. Do you remember how you met him?

Locke: Joe couldn't cast this one part for Kansas City, Hank—I called him the horny truck driver. Well, he couldn't find the right man for the part. And he went and saw *Dreamer*; and saw me in it, and said, "That's Hank." But he couldn't find me—I was out in the desert. He found me, brought me to M-G-M, because that's where his partner, Sam Gage, worked. So there I was walking through the soundstages of M-G-M. I walked out on the set of *Coma*—that's where I met Sam Gage. We went back to his office and he said, "Sure that's Hank." I got $500 for doing it.

Manshots: How did you get along with Steve Boyd?

Locke: Got along very well with him. He's straight, y'know. Big dick. He was supposed to fuck me, but he's straight, so he doesn't fuck me, but he puts it between my legs, and we get the scene off.

Manshots: How did you like working with Jack Wrangler?

Locke: Jack Wrangler was a star at the time and I was a nobody. So it was real nice working with him, all along the line. He was real professional. I got along fine with him.

Manshots: Did you have any idea at the beginning that *Kansas City* would end up a trilogy?

Locke: I thought it was a loop. (*He laughs*) I had no idea I was going to be the star. And I didn't know they were going to advertise it the way they did. My brother called my mother and said, "Did you see your son's picture in the paper?" She said, "No, what have you been doing, son?" He said, "Not me—your other son." She said, "Oh, my God, what's he done now?" (*Roars with laughter*)

Manshots: Where are you from?

Locke: I'm from Oakland.

Manshots: So you've been around this area most of your life.

Locke: I picked prunes for my first pair of Levi's right here on the base of the Russian River. This is my home.

Manshots: Tell us about the shooting of *Kansas City*.

Locke: I thought it was going to be shown in porno stores. And then, all of a sudden, I became a star overnight. (*Snaps fingers*) Just like that.

Manshots: When did you first know you were a star?

Locke: When I walked down Christopher Street in New York City, and a guy walked into a parking meter looking at me.

Manshots: Do you have any memories of the shooting of *Kansas City*?

Locke: One day Joe said, "We have this piss scene." And I said, "Well, I'm not really into that, because it's degrading, I think." I'm gay and I'm proud, and I don't like degradation, but I rationalized that if the guy wants it and likes it, why not? It's only degrading if you make it degrading. So I said, "Yeah, I'll do it." So, the night of the shoot, we went over there and Joe says, "Ice box is full of beer, and we're not gonna shoot the piss scene till later, so why don't you start drinking?" It's about six o'clock in the evening, and about eight, I really have to piss. And Joe says, "Well, Richard, we're not really ready for it yet. Why don't you take a piss and start drinking more beer?" So I only do half a piss, 'cause I want to do a good scene. So about ten o'clock, I've really got to go, but Joe says, "Well, we're not ready yet, so go piss some more." So I do another half-piss. By this time, I'm sloshed, just drunker than a skunk, and wondering how I'm gonna do a good scene if I'm drunk. About one in the morning, I'm sloshed to the gills, can't see, everything is blurry, and I can feel the piss up to my eyeballs. Joe finally sets up the scene, and I piss and I piss and I piss and I piss—I pissed so much, I couldn't believe it.

Manshots: When did Joe tell you *Kansas City* was going to be a trilogy?

Locke: Well, I can't remember now. I didn't make but $500 on the first film, and when I found out there was going to be a second and third, I thought I'd better cool it on asking for more money for the second, but after the second one, I'd get him on the third. (*Chuckles*) I did much better on the second, *El Paso*, but when it came time to do the third, I said, "I want $8,000 and a percentage." Sam had been working in Hollywood a long time, and he knew the difference between net and gross. I didn't. So they talked me into $2,500 and five per cent of the net. There's no such thing as net, so I got five per cent of nothing.

Manshots: Did you know Fred Halsted before the shooting of *El Paso?*

Locke: I met Fred at the San Francisco Art Institute when they were showing his film, *L.A. Plays Itself.* After the screening, Fred came out on the stage with—what's was his lover's name, Joey?—and he bopped him all the way across the stage, and then asked for questions from the audience. I thought, "What kind of man is this?" 'Cause I'm gay and I'm proud. I don't believe in bopping people. And I'd read interviews with him, and he sounded like a very rough man. And I didn't know if I wanted to make a film with Fred Halsted. I just didn't like the image. Well, he was a teddy bear in real life. A wonderful, caring, beautiful teddy bear.

Manshots: Well, you certainly had an onscreen rapport.

Locke: My best acting scene, I think, was at the end of the film, where we parted. It was the best scene I'd done, except maybe for the scene in *Kansas City* where the big, huge cock came through the bedsprings. That was pure art.

Manshots: Do you remember shooting that scene?

Locke: I remember the man was an older man. It was the most erotic scene I'd seen up to that point in films. To me, it was very erotic, very classy, quite something. I remember how extraordinary the cock was, I remember how I loved it.

Manshots: Moving on to *L.A. Tool & Die*, tell us some more about Will Seagers.

Locke: I'd heard the guy I was gonna be with was really stupendous. So I took off for San Francisco about a month before the film was about to start. I thought I'd work out a little bit and try to quit smoking. Every time I wanted a cigarette, I'd go to the gym. And I joined a gym on Market Street, and Will was one of the instructors. And he said he had a friend who wanted to produce a film. That was *Cruising the Castro*. To this day, I don't know how Joe found out about it. I told him, "Don't get mad at me, I didn't know he was Will Seagers. " But he was afraid we'd ruined the chemistry by working together already.

Manshots: You hadn't.

Locke: There was a magic between Will and me, and that happens very rarely onscreen. But he had this thing with me—every time we had a scene together, we came at the same time, just like the honeymoon couple. There was a magic.

Manshots: Was it limited strictly to onscreen?

Locke: Yeah. He had a lover. (*Pause*) He had the most extraordinary asshole. It would open and close like the lens of a camera. (*Laughs*) I'd never seen anything like it. (*Pause*) But there was a chemistry onscreen. I asked about offscreen, and he said, "No, I have a little lover, and I'm happy." So there was no offscreen magic. I lived in the desert and he lived in San Francisco, and every once in awhile I'd see him when I was in San Francisco. As for fraternizing or going out to the bars and stuff like that, we never did that. In fact, I never did that with any of them.

Manshots: Another director who played an important part in your career was Arthur Bressan, Jr.

Locke: (*Softly*) Artie ... gorgeous ... extraordinary. (*Pause*) I attended a Gay Film Festival in a church on Geary Street somewhere around 1966 or thereabouts. I saw a little eighteen-minute film done on Super 8, in black and white, made in New York, called "Boys." About two young men who fell in love in a playground in New York City. It was an extraordinary film, especially for its time. I had to talk to the director afterwards, and I did. And that's the first time I met Artie. And we sort of struck up a friendship, and our friendship went on from that point. Artie filmed me at different times. One time he wanted to do a film of *Billy Budd*. We had some footage from that and some other things. From Gay Pride Parades—the very first one in San Francisco. It's in *Gay USA*, and there's also footage of me in *Passing Strangers*. Actually, I didn't do it for *Passing Strangers*—the footage just wound up in it. Then one day Artie came to me and said, "Listen, I've written this screenplay. It includes some of the footage we've done together and we're going to shoot some new stuff. This screenplay, I call it *plorno*—porno with a plot. And what I want to do is show this rugged exterior you have as opposed to this loving interior. I want to contrast that." So he really wrote *Forbidden Letters* just for me.

Manshots: Do you remember much about your co-star, Robert Adams?

Locke: We didn't have the chemistry Will Seagers and I had, but it worked out. I've never been one to go for a younger person. I generally stick with people my own age or thereabouts. I was real awkward in that situation. (*At that moment, John, his hunky younger lover, passes through the room on his way to take a shower.*) I still find myself in that awkward situation today. (*Chuckles*) I didn't set out to get John. We just fell in love. I never had it in my mind to be a daddy to a younger man. Never. Never entered my mind. Although I knew Artie always had that in mind.

Manshots: Oh, very much so.

Locke: Very much so.

Manshots: The most famous scene in *Forbidden Letters* was the jail scene, which was actually shot on location in Alcatraz. How did you ever pull that off?

Locke: Well, it was strange. I was talking to Artie, and I said, "Artie, how are you going to possibly shoot on Alcatraz?" He said, "Simple—we'll just say we're students." I said, "Artie, you're thirty-five years old." Well, it worked. They were shooting Clint Eastwood's *Escape from Alcatraz* at the same time. So there we were, Hollywood on one side of the penitentiary and this little "student shoot" on the other side. We were in an abandoned section of the prison, but the tourist groups were still coming through. Every time they'd come through, we'd stop shooting. Well, you know Alcatraz is right there in the middle of the channel, and you have these cold winds coming off the Pacific, and there were no windows in this place—total iron and cement. It was the coldest place I've ever been in in my entire life. To stand there without shaking, and jack off, and try to keep it sexy was probably the most difficult thing I've ever done, even for those people sitting out there in the dark. (*A soft laugh*)

Manshots: So, in a way, Artie directed both your first film appearance and your last.

Locke: I'd like to say one more thing about *Forbidden Letters*. We filmed it over a period of five years. Some of the shots in there were over five years old by the time it was released. We started working on it long before *Dreamer*, so in a way it was my first picture. It just sort of evolved. It was a very extraordinary movie. My most favorite movie. The acting in it was superb. (*He chuckles, embarrassed.*) Not to blow my own horn, but it was superb. But that was because I was being directed by a great director. I don't think we'll ever realize how great Artie was, and the saddest thing, I think, was that Artie's best work was in front of him. Artie had a way of having a social consciousness intertwined with porno. It was not porno, it was erotica.

Manshots: Another important director you worked for was Steve Scott in *Gemini*, again with Jack Wrangler.

Locke: It was shot in L.A. I fucked Jack on a pool table—one of my fantasies. I've since fucked people on pool tables, but I remember that one. I'll always wonder what a "nice boy like him" was doing getting fucked on a pool table. (*Snorts*) In joke.

Manshots: Do you remember the film, *Pool Party*, for Toby Ross? Joe Gage told me that was the film he saw you in, not *Dreamer*.

Locke: No, the one he saw was *Dreamer*.

Manshots: I'm sure he said *Pool Party*. At the Adonis.

Locke: I don't remember. But I do remember when *Pool Party* was done, I was living in L.A. When we went out to do the pool sequence, it was the first time I'd ever fisted anybody. And that footage was never put in the finished film. God knows whatever happened to it. I'd like to see that sequence, because it was the first time I ever stuck my hand in anybody's body—and it was on film.

Manshots: Another important director for whom you've worked is Wakefield Poole—in *Take One*, which is one of the most interesting films, and the only one not on video, I believe.

Locke: Tied up in litigation by the guy he made it with. (*Pause*) The way Wake did it was he selected the people he wanted to be in the film, and then he called them in and interviewed them on camera, and asked them what their fantasy was—and then he made it happen. My fantasy was to fuck my lover on the roof of my house in the desert with my windmill in the background. Wakefield is a genius. Not in the same mold that Artie was a genius, or not in the same mold that Joe Gage was a genius. But they all had something going for them. I had the privilege to work for some of the finest.

Manshots: The critics generally consider *Heatstroke* to be your greatest film.

Locke: Yeah, I would agree with that. *Forbidden Letters* is my favorite film, because of working with Artie—there are personal reasons. But *Heatstroke* has its favorite place, too.

Manshots: Tell us about Roy Garrett.

Locke: I liked Roy. He wasn't my style. Y'know, a lot of times, you're paired with someone that is not to your liking—in the sense that some people like apples, some people like oranges, and that doesn't mean apples are rotten. And Roy was right there and doing what he was supposed to do in a great way.

Manshots: How about the scene with the marine, Clay Russell?

Locke: Oh, Clay's one of my favorite people. I've made two movies with him. I made *El Paso*, in which he played a park ranger, and this one where he played a marine. You can't seem to get him out of a uniform. (*Snickers*) I always did. He's got great tits.

Manshots: Tell us about your fiftieth birthday.

Locke: I celebrated by climbing the second largest mountain in the United States. It was Mt. Albert in Colorado—14,480 feet. Admittedly, the next day I stayed in bed, but I climbed the mountain. Y'know, I went to a positive support group one time, and I didn't see much positive support there because everybody was whining. One guy said, "I wanted to go to Bora Bora." And my reaction was: "Why don't you go to Bora Bora—there's nothing stopping you." You've gotta be happy, think happy, do those things that you've always wanted to do. I have a Fundamentalist background, and Jerry Falwell has said that AIDS is God plucking his weeds. And I tend to think it's more God taking his most lovely blooms. Several times in my life, I've felt I overstayed, because I've had to sit and watch my friends go one by one by one. In 1989, I got very sick because I let my mind go, and the will to die outweighed the will to live. I wanted to be with my friends.

Luckily, I got out of it. Actually, I hit bottom in 1989, but then I started getting out. I've always been a fighter, and the thing to do is fight, to have that will to live, to fight the disease.

Manshots: Are you happy these days?

Locke: Yeah, for the most part.

Manshots: What is your life like these days?

Locke: Well, I don't work. I think work brings on too much stress. My job right now is to stay well, and I have an income from disability.

Manshots: Richard, I have no sense that I've spent the day today with an unhealthy man, with a man who is about to die.

Locke: Hmm . . . Well, you know the nice thing about film is that I will live a long time, even after I die. 'Cause it's there.▼

THE FILMS OF RICHARD LOCKE

Dreamer (1975)
Sins of Johnny X (1975)
Pool Party (1975)
Two Days in a Hot Place (1975)
Passing Strangers (1975)
Forbidden Letters (1976)
Kansas City Trucking Co. (1976)
Take One (1977)
El Paso Wrecking Corp. (1977)
Gemini (1978)
L.A. Tool & Die (1979)
Cruisin' the Castro (1981)
Sixty Niner (1982)
Best of the Superstars (1982)
Heatstroke (1982)
Daddy Dearest (1984)